MOONWALKING

PRAISE FOR *MOONWALKING*

"This novel in verse, alternately narrated by two boys in 1980s Greenpoint, Brooklyn . . . eloquently tackles race, culture and life on the spectrum."

—*THE NEW YORK TIMES*

★ "The coauthors' equally strong contributions evocatively bring the characters and setting to life through visual poetry. The even pacing makes for an engrossing read, and the characters' pain and promise will remain with readers. A stellar, hauntingly beautiful narrative."

—*KIRKUS REVIEWS*, STARRED REVIEW

★ "In an authentic look at the racial divide that continues today, authors Elliott and Miller-Lachmann bring varying degrees of . . . authenticity to the characterizations and emotions represented. Their multilayered exposure of a specific time in history will resonate with modern readers, who will see these racist acts echoed all too loudly in current events."

—*BOOKLIST*, STARRED REVIEW

★ "A tender, engrossing tribute to art and close interpersonal bonds that explores themes of neurodivergence, mental health, and institutional prejudice."

—*PUBLISHERS WEEKLY*, STARRED REVIEW

★ "Through alternating first-person accounts, and with varied poetic styles, Elliott and Miller-Lachmann present a thoughtfully structured and sensitively rendered verse novel set in early-1980s Brooklyn featuring two memorable protagonists... Both authors are adept at evocatively re-creating the setting, with references ranging from Ronald Reagan's anti-union stance to Jean-Michel Basquiat, Michael Jackson, and the Clash. Authors' notes give background on various aspects of the novel, including autism as a likely diagnosis for JJ, using today's terms."

—*THE HORN BOOK*, STARRED REVIEW

MOON

ZETTA ELLIOTT   LYN MILLER-LACHMANN

WALKING

SQUARE
FISH

FARRAR STRAUS GIROUX
NEW YORK

SQUARE
FISH

An imprint of Macmillan Publishing Group, LLC
120 Broadway, New York, NY 10271 • mackids.com

Square Fish and the Square Fish logo are trademarks of Macmillan and
are used by Farrar Straus Giroux under license from Macmillan.

Our books may be purchased in bulk for promotional, educational,
or business use. Please contact your local bookseller or the Macmillan
Corporate and Premium Sales Department at (800) 221-7945 ext. 5442
or by email at MacmillanSpecialMarkets@macmillan.com.

The Library of Congress has cataloged the hardcover edition as follows:
Names: Elliott, Zetta, author. | Miller-Lachmann, Lyn, 1956– author.
Title: Moonwalking / Zetta Elliott, Lyn Miller-Lachmann.
Description: First edition. | New York: Farrar Straus Giroux Books for Young
    Readers, 2022. | Audience: Ages 10–14 | Audience: Grades 7–9 | Summary:
    In 1980s Brooklyn, new student JJ Pankowski, an autistic, punk-rock
    lover, befriends Pie Velez, an Afro-Latinx math geek and graffiti artist.
Identifiers: LCCN 2021015591 | ISBN 9780374314378 (hardcover)
Subjects: CYAC: Novels in verse. | Friendship—Fiction. | Autism—Fiction. |
    Identity—Fiction. | Brooklyn (New York, N.Y.)—History—20th century—Fiction.
Classification: LCC PZ7.5.E44 Mo 2022 | DDC [Fic]—dc23
LC record available at https://lccn.loc.gov/2021015591

Originally published in the United States by Farrar Straus Giroux
First Square Fish edition, 2023
Book designed by Liz Dresner
Square Fish logo designed by Filomena Tuosto
Printed in the United States of America by
Lakeside Book Company, Harrisonburg, Virginia

ISBN 978-1-250-86651-6
10 9 8 7 6 5 4 3 2 1

MOONWALKING

41592653589793238462643383279$

1

.

3

Kids call me Pie—
cherry though I'm
maybe not so sweet
a flag in my window
five stripes with only
pollo with platanos
creamy tembleque
room left in my belly
at home I'm Pierre
really know what a
mad if she found the
my bag when night
spray my sign leave
so folks know I was
to do the right thing
with her homework
easy for Pilar like it
her blue eyes check
that runs down her
got different daddies
before I was born he's
moreno *Papi*'s just a
nothing to me no

PIE

9

5

4197169399375105820974944

not like apple or
just as American
proud Boricua got
red white and blue
one star arroz con
is my favorite meal
for dessert if there's
I'm Pie at school but
'cause Mami don't
tag is and she'd be
can of paint I tote in
falls I hit the street
my mark on walls
there at home I try
help my little sister
'cause school ain't
is for me folks see
the long blond hair

back and know we
mine took off right   now
  the reason they call me   here
    word that don't mean   around
      more I'm the only man

NIGHT FLIGHT

I

Dad says the bank owns our house now.
He hands me one box from the liquor store.
"Fill it with whatever you plan to take, JJ.
Leave everything else behind.
Don't
tell
anyone."

I have no one
            to tell
and Dad
            knows it.

II

Last summer we stood by the Nassau Expressway
which connected my home
            Lynbrook, Long Island
                        and JFK airport

me and my dad
      together
holding screen-printed signs
with the union bug
PATCO AIR TRAFFIC CONTROLLERS
his said
MY DADDY IS ON STRIKE
mine said.

Someone chucked an egg
that flew through exhaust-broiled air
and—*splat!*—broke across Dad's knuckles
spilled its insides
all over his sign.

Why would they do this to us?
We were standing up for *them*.

I sucked back snot in my throat.
"Don't you go crying, JJ,"
Dad said,
and I dared not in front of him
or his union brothers
even though
slowly hardening yolk
wiped out his *P*.

P for *PATCO*.
P for *Pankowski*.
P for our place in the world.

III

It took three days to break the strike.
Six months to realize
no place would
hire Dad
again.

They called it
blacklisted.

One year for us to go broke
with no one working.

Now Mom packs my clothes in a suitcase
summer tees and a winter coat.

This is not a vacation
but a trip back in time
a reversal

from Lynbrook
to Brooklyn

where Dad fled from Poland
with Babcia and Dziadek
when he was twelve.

IV

Wedged in the back seat
of Uncle Russell's Toyota
(our car sold for cash
so the bank wouldn't take it too)
we cross not oceans but highways.

I squeeze Mom's hand
between boxes and suitcases.
Streetlamps flicker past
like summer's fireflies
like a movie rewound.

An airplane screeches overhead
and zooms in for a landing
one of the night flights
that Dad used to help bring home.

Now *we're* a night flight
fleeing our home in darkness . . .

V

In my box is:

Casio keyboard
Walkman
headphones
punk-rock cassettes
  packed like a jigsaw puzzle
a Clash poster
zines
a red-and-white SOLIDARNOŚĆ banner
wrapped around *The Chocolate War*
  to protect
  the cover
  fragile pages

        me and Jerry
        alone and bullied
        Dad in mourning
        the whole world
        against us

Do I dare disturb the universe?

BOMB

rattle
rattle
rattle
hissssssssssssssssssss

till I met Ricky
I never knew mist
wrapped in metal could be
light as air and dark as night
or brighter than a neon sign
I shake the can and
the seed of a rainbow clatters
inside before blooming in my palm
and climbing across the wall
like the unruly roses in
Tito's garden
here in the barrio
tags spread like wildfire
we write in code on concrete
words most folks can't read
signs that wow
warn and
won't be ignored
WE ARE HERE
you can't erase us
you can close your eyes
or look away
try to scrub off the Sharpie
but we'll just scratch our
names into glass
eternal
you can paint over our tags

                    but we won't go away
                    we'll just wait till night falls
                    and throw up another
                    BOMB

it's all in the wrist
that's what Ricky told me
hold the can loose
but press down hard on the nozzle
till the paint flows in a steady spray
Ricky let me watch and learn
as he bombed bodega walls
and storefront steel doors
we scaled fire escapes and
water towers protected by
height and the drama that
unfolds in the street at night
no one thinks to look up but
cops cruise down the block
so you gotta work fast
Ricky used to time me
till I could make a decent tag
in ten seconds or less
my name is Pierre but
it takes less time to
spray Pie on a wall
Ricky said I was too young
to join his crew but
he schooled me anyway
let me tag along unless
he was bombing the MTA
Ricky looked out for me
he was the only brother
I ever had and now he's gone
a cross sprayed on the sidewalk marks
the spot where he got shot down

RIP RICKY
shot in the back at fifteen
shot walking *away* from a fight
just like he taught me to do

crews are still out here
battling
besting
busting the alphabet
breaking the law
bombing the bloque
with color so fresh
and styles so cold
can't nobody hold us back

Mami tells me it's wrong to
deface private property
like the buildings we tag
are clean as the Taj Mahal
ain't no palaces round here
but Mami acts like a little paint
makes things worse than they
already are
she still stitches my name
on the tags of my clothes
but nothing in the 'hood
belongs to me or ever will
good, Mami says, then it
won't be hard for you
to leave the barrio
this wasn't meant to be
our home forever
but Mami's plans fell through
once she had me and now
we're stuck here until

I can find a way to
move us out

I need my own plan
Mateo joined the army
when he turned eighteen
and came home from Vietnam
without a scratch on him
but Tía Rosa still says it was
the war that killed my cousin
not the needle they found
in his arm

nobody dropped a
BOMB
on Williamsburg but
it still feels like a war zone out here
buildings burning crumbling boarded up
till the junkies move in and start doing their dirty deals
little kids shouldn't have to see that mess
sometimes I get so mad I feel
like I'm about to explode

but Ms. Kirschbaum says
art is a weapon
art is a tool
art can be the balm that heals
all wounds
art won't bring Ricky back
but Ms. K says a kid
not much older than me
half Puerto Rican / half Haitian
started out on the street
with a spray can in his hand
now SAMO© has his pieces

in galleries and magazines
he's worldwide
legit
a real artist making bank
getting paid to do in a studio
what we do in the street for free
I want to know
is his mother proud of him
if I paint on canvas instead of concrete
will Mami smile at me again
will the line between her eyes disappear
will the voices in her head go away
I don't want to let her down
when she's got such high hopes for me
Pilar counts on me too so I can't
afford to have a short fuse
I can't detonate or implode
put my fist in somebody's face
or catch a bullet in my back
for now I keep a can in my bag
and when my homework's done
I go up on the roof to work
on the piece Ricky didn't get to finish
maybe one day something I've made
will hang in a museum
but until I blow up
I'll keep making throw-ups
so folks in my 'hood can say
we knew him when . . .

rattle
rattle
rattle
hisssssssssssssssssssss

THREE CHORDS

It's half past midnight
when we pull up to the row house
back seat and trunk
stuffed with our things

but after we unload—
in silence, so neighbors won't see
once proud union family
sneaking home
whipped, tails tucked—

a guitar and amp
remain next to the wheel well
the final item in Pandora's box:
Hope.

It's a Fender Telecaster
same guitar Joe Strummer
plays for the Clash
his spray-painted black
this one red and white
like the Polish flag
like the SOLIDARNOŚĆ banner
that hung on my wall
and protected my book
The Chocolate War.

"This was my first guitar, Joey.
Now it's gonna be yours,"
Uncle Russell whispers
as Dad and Mom

talk with Babcia
in Dad's old room
in this low-ceilinged basement flat
that stinks of wet carpet and bleach
and not-my-home.

He's the only one who calls me Joey
and it sounds like *joy*
Uncle Russell not really my uncle
but a Cockney from East London
punk rock in his blood
union strong
the one who held the megaphone
when we stood at the Nassau Expressway
chanting, singing union songs
dodging taunts
and eggs

                    him most of all
                    the troublemaker
                    the ringleader
                    the foreigner in
                    President Reagan's land.

Uncle Russell spends the rest of the night
teaching me three chords
in Babcia's living room

                    the front room
                    where I'm supposed
                    to sleep
                    if I could sleep

C, D, G,
squeezing my fingertips into knife-sharp strings
his fingers calloused and rough.
"The more you practice
the tougher
your fingertips will get,"
he says.

My fingers trip over the strings
muffle the chords
release *thuds* instead of *twangs*
instead of a tune
a *clang.*

When I packed my Casio keyboard,
Mom said, "Leave it behind, JJ.
It's a waste of space
and you can't make noise
at your Babcia's place."

And I remember what
the piano teacher at my old school said,
"He won't be the next Chopin,"
but I brought the keyboard anyway
and I'm practicing this guitar
till my fingers bleed

because in this punk zine
Sniffin' Glue

                                one that I swiped
                                from Alina

Joe Strummer said
you don't need talent
you don't need skill
all you need is a loud voice
an electric guitar
three chords
and a story.

MISSING ALINA

Left behind on Long Island
like our house and furniture
my board games and LEGO bricks
is my sister
Alina
who taught me to dribble a basketball
wait for my turn
punch a bully smack on the nose.

She said there's no room for her
in Brooklyn.
The basketball team needs its point guard
the honor society its treasurer
Claire O'Keefe her best friend.

I wish I had a best friend to stay with
a full scholarship
a place on the team.

Maybe Brooklyn is your place, JJ,
she said
the day
before our night flight.
And when you're not
just
my kid brother
you'll become
the person you're meant to be.

I pat down my hair where she used to ruffle it.

Even if she's right
my family's the chair I sit on
and leaving her behind
kicks one of the
                    legs
                    right
                    out
                    from
                    under
me.

SUGARLAND

there is sweetness in Los Sures
some days when the wind blows off the river
you can even taste azúcar in the air
sugar crystals crushed to dust
float on the breeze and
coat the clothes and eyelashes of
all the workers in the Domino factory
the Sugar House they call it

a tree grows in Brooklyn but
sugarcane sprouts in the Caribbean
and then leaves like we do
crosses the sea and gets ground up in this city
by machines running all day and night
just to make life a bit sweeter for everyone else
Mami says once upon a time on our island
people like us cut sugarcane by hand
with machetes sharpened by stones and
swung beneath a sweltering sun

out here
on my bloque
blades cut other things
this ain't no *West Side Story*
with blanquitos pretending
to be Boricuas
it's true—we got our own gangs
turf wars & tragedies
hearts break and bodies bleed
yet we still find reasons to dance in the street
on the way home from the store

my face on fire from the food stamps Mami used
we pass three old-timers making music
not 'cause they have to, just 'cause they can
one plays the flute, another strikes a guiro
and the third taps the bongos with wrinkled brown fingers
their tune teases a smile from Mami's lips
the rhythm loosens everybody's hips
and soon there's a party right there on the sidewalk
shame forgotten I take the bag of groceries from Mami
and Pilar claps a hand over her mouth to keep the giggles inside
as a viejo pulls our mother into his arms
cradles her like she is made of glass
and then twirls her como una reina at a cotillón

meanwhile down the bloque
B-boys pop and lock
as a boom box blasts beats & rhymes
emcees flow over scratched-up tracks
and bodies bend but never break
kids not much older than me
battle on sheets of cardboard laid over concrete
I watch them wheel their legs like windmills
spin on their skullies
float over the ground as if

                                    on the

                  they're walking   moon

Los Sures is full of music
it pours into the street from passing cars
and open bedroom windows
it rains down on us free as water
from a hydrant on a hot summer's day
music brings relief, release
we soak ourselves
catch droplets on our tongues
because there is just as much sweetness

in Mami's boleros
as there is in Pilar's coquito
scooped cold from Jose's creaking carrito
and for me—all the sugarcane in the world
couldn't be as sweet as a shy smile
or secret wave from Benita
when her father looks
the other way

life isn't easy in Los Sures
we may get beat down
ground up and sacked
but we are not defeated
life can sometimes be bitter
there is still sweetness here

PUBLIC SCHOOL

I

Middle school a number:
                    126
Four-story building takes up the whole block.
How will I find my classroom
change rooms before the late bell rings
avoid shoves from behind
                    feet outstretched?

I have no choice
no Catholic school scholarship like Alina.
It's public school for me.

Why couldn't I have fit in
followed the rules
even if I didn't understand
        or believe them
made a team
gotten A's on my report cards
        instead of C's
because I read books I wanted
like *The Chocolate War*
instead of the ones the teachers assigned?

                    A book is a book, right?

Everyone here is a stranger
everyone with dark hair
        like mine
but as I draw closer

I see their faces
        a hundred shades
                of brown

and across the street
under a tree
a tight circle
of white faces
close to each other
apart from the rest
their expressions
tough
grim
ready.

Do I go to them?
                        Is that where I belong?
With the faces of kids
who messed with me since kindergarten
        or else stood by and watched.

I turn away from them
pass through the sea of
        brown
        browner
        brownest

Do they see my hands shake
throat close, heartbeat stutter
knees wobble as I step inside?

Does my blood drain to my feet
        no fight
        no flight
        face pale . . .

white
whiter
whitest . . .

ghost

II

In homeroom
the only other person
who looks like me
is the teacher.

She stumbles over
        Narvaez
        Ortiz-Irrizarry
        Pumarejo
and the kids shout out
            laugh
            or argue
            with her:
"My name.
Don't tell me how
to pronounce it."

She has no problem with
        Pankowski
(even pronounces the *w* as *v*).

When she calls me
I only raise my hand
imagine she sees me.
            I cannot speak
            much less tell her

I go by JJ
not Joseph John.

Nobody notices me
and that's the way
I need it.

INVISIBLE ME

One week later
they still haven't noticed
                    me.

I watch them.
Black
Brown
White
                    from afar
grateful.

They're a team
I won't go out for.
A party
for which
I don't beg
an invitation.

                    A universe
                    I dare
                    not
                    disturb.

Except for the call
that comes
to Dad
at home
in the afternoon.
His face goes

red:

"What do you mean
he hasn't been
in class? We send him
every
single
morning."

redder:

"Skipping classes? He's had
his problems
but skipping class
was never
one
of them."

reddest:

"I don't know where he goes.
You bet I'll be there first thing
tomorrow with him."

Click!
Slam!

"JJ, come here right now!"

His palm smacks my cheek.
Glasses fly.
Face stings.
Teeth throb.
Eyelids burn.

No! Can't cry
or he'll give me

even more
to cry about.

"I went to every class
every day." I try
not to whimper.

                              Wimp.
"I'll
show
you."

I dash to my corner
my box
flip through my notebooks
show him notes
homework
the "Do Now" that begins each class:

Write a sentence using one word
we defined yesterday.
At high <u>latitude</u> the nights are short in summer
and long in winter.

                    We live in a high latitude.
                    Is this my family's winter?

This time he believes me
doesn't hit me again
doesn't say he's sorry either
can't send me to my room
because it's Babcia's
        living room.

Next day
he shows the dean my notebooks.

"My boy was in all his classes
and your teachers didn't see him?"

"Thirty-five in a class, Mr. Pankowski.
Sometimes it's hard
to keep track," she says.

My last school had sixteen.

The dean looks my way.
I avoid her eyes
cover my ears to muffle
the whirring fan
blowing nothing
except
hot air.

"Joseph John . . ."

"It's JJ," I mumble.
Gaze fixed on too-tight sneakers
duct tape wrapped across one toe.

"JJ."
        She stops.
                        Starts.
"Has anyone bullied you?"

I shake my head
sit on my hands
to keep from touching
my throbbing cheek.

Not here.
Not yet.

SPEAK UP

"Son, you need to speak up,"
Dad says
with a trace of the accent
he never lost
from the old country
where
*Children should be seen
and not heard.*

I freeze
confused
cannot speak
now
in the echoey
chipped-tile lobby
any more than
then
in the dean's office
sweaty butt smashed against
orange plastic chair
useless fan
scrambling
all
       the
             words.

My mind yells out
those words unspoken
while it rummages for
my invisible list:

Things That Make No Sense

Speak up

                    Shut up

Put up your dukes
show bullies you mean business

                    Ignore the bullies
                    and they'll go away

Family means everything

                    No one says Alina's name

Marriage is forever
for better, for worse
for richer, for poorer

                    Does Babcia hear
                    Mom and Dad fight at night
                    from her bedroom like I do?

Women stay home
and take care of
their kids

                    Mom and Babcia
                    clean apartments
                    across the river

Men get a job
and support
their family

                    Dad sits home all day
                    can't find a job
                    because he spoke up

You should start a union
go out on strike
fight for your rights

If you work for
Reagan's government
you have no rights

Fight for freedom
unfurl your red-and-white banner
call yourself
Solidarność

Do what they tell you
don't speak up
don't walk the picket line
don't sing

Solidarity forever
for the union makes us strong . . .

I wave the hall pass from the office.
"Dad, I have to get to class now.
I'll see you at home,

okay?"

what if the next Einstein looks like me / what if the cure for cancer is boxed up in the brain of a brother locked up just for tagging a train / ain't nobody more creative than a kid with no money in his pockets but a dream in his heart / that's why I make art / empty hands don't always mean an empty head / they say necessity is the mother of invention but half of us are stuck in detention just for refusing to dim our shine / Zullo ain't blind he just refuses to see how brilliant I could be 'cause he's too busy playing chess in our classroom / moving the white kids up and knocking Black kids like me off the board / he'd rather see us stealing bases / throwing touchdowns or winning races / it's cool if you can handle a ball but that's not all we're good for / I want something more / shouldn't have to wave my hand in his face but that's the only way to make Zullo see me / I insist on an A instead of a B / not trying to coast / gotta make the most of my time in school / sure I got jokes but that don't make me a fool / I got talent that just can't be denied / not saying I'm a genius (yet) but you can bet I know a whole lot more than some kids who only got through the door because of their color / me being an honor student means a lot to my mother / sets a good example for Pilar / and I bet it'd make my dad proud too if he knew I was striving / steady climbing that mountain so I can plant my flag at the top / check out the view / pull someone else up behind me if they need a hand / or two

GENIUS

MORE THINGS THAT
MAKE NO SENSE

I

My schedule has *H* after the subject
and kids don't change
from class to class

only the rooms change
and the teachers change.

There's this genius kid
                              Pierre Velez.

He calls himself Pi
not like the pie that you eat
but the mathematical symbol
that stands for 3.14 and
a whole lot of numbers that follow
that never end.

Pi's arm shoots up with every question
skinniest brownest arm
like a raised banner
fingers scraping the sky.
None of that timid half-mast maybe.

"Let's give someone else a chance
to answer," teacher says
and, yes, these kids
know the answers.

I'm a half
                              step behind,
            the backbeat
to a song I've never heard before.

H stands for *honors*.
It takes me a week
to figure this out.

Me: C student at my old school
not even second best
but good enough to move from
grade to grade
                  understanding half.

My old school called it
"pervasive developmental disorder"   translation   "stupid"
"learning disabilities"   translation   "lazy"
"poor large-motor skills"   translation   "clumsy"
"poor verbal skills"   translation   "shy"
"poor social skills"   translation   "weird"

And my glasses?
Kids used to call me nerd
knocked them off when
I passed in the hallway
but they only made me look smart.

II

At dinner I ask Mom
show her my schedule card

                              because Dad doesn't care
                              doesn't think I'm going to college
                              doesn't think I need college.

I tell her about Pi
and the other brown hands
waving in the air.

"You grew up on Long Island.
You went to Catholic school.
The work was harder
so you're much better prepared
        than they are."

I punch my fork into the last of my pierogies
push it around my plate
in a melted butter circle
its circumference
widest distance from end to end

                              even though a circle
                              has no beginning
                              and no end

multiplied by pi.

Pi explained it in class
and for the first time
I understood.

And while thinking about math
there's another for my list of
                    Things
                    That
                    Make
                    No
                    Sense.

One out of twenty kids
            in the school
but one out of four kids
            in honors class

is white

like me.

PAPI (TRICUBE)

me, Mami
and Pilar
just us three

together
forever
trinity

not holy
but still whole
without him

LOLA'S SMILE

before she was my mother
Mami was Maria Antonia Velez
first in our family to go to college
she didn't live in a dorm
but Mami told me that
taking the train into Manhattan
felt like riding a rocket up to the moon
where there's zero gravity

Mami said that's how she felt
whenever she stepped on campus
or sat in a classroom where every word
written on the board and inside the textbook
was about *her* people *her* island *her* culture
she was never shamed for speaking Spanish
because the professors spoke it too
for the first time Mami read poems
written in her mother tongue
fell in love with one poet's words and so

took her name to keep the feeling
and her memory
alive

Tía Rosa still calls Mami "Maria"
(*Why not? It's good enough for la madre de Jesús*)
but everyone else calls my mother
Lola

that's who she was when my father
flew across the Atlantic to study in New York
their campus was the whole city
and they shared the same friends
the same struggle
they felt the same pride in roots
buried too deep for too long
at the university in Kinshasa my father
studied in French but Mami said he spoke
better English than most Americans

What was his mother tongue?

it's one of those questions Mami struggles to answer
so I go to the library but the musty encyclopedia tells me
folks speak over two hundred languages in Zaire
when I tell Mami she gets upset
Don't call it that—your father never called it that
but when I ask why she just sighs and rubs her temples
I'm telling you the things that matter, mijo
your father loved his people so much . . .

she says that every time she holds the faded
Polaroid I keep in my sketchbook
I never heard his voice but I see love
in the way my father's arm wraps around

Mami's shoulders pulling her close
he smiles at the camera though his dark eyes
are hidden by darker sunglasses
nothing in his face in that moment suggests
he's the type of dude to make a baby
and then bounce but he did

it is 1970
Mami rests her head against his neck
her blue eyes turned up with a saint's adoration
on her lips a soft smile that only returns
when she holds that Polaroid
I bring it out sometimes
when the attacks make Mami
forget who we are

he loved you, too, Mami
I try to remind her
but she always corrects me

us—mijo
your father loved us

RONNIE RAYGUN

When I write my song   my story
it will be about how much
I hate Ronald Reagan

or Ronnie Raygun
which is what the zines I swiped from Alina
call him.

Wrinkle-faced old man with dyed hair.
Washed-up Hollywood actor.
Comic book villain pretending to be the hero.

His ray gun zapped:
Dad's union   Dad's job
Our house   Our family
          Our life.

How can he zap Dad's union
and claim to be the superhero
defending Solidarity?

Reagan's on our side,
Mom said.
Dad told me he was president
of the actors' union
then decided to be president
for all of us.

Mom and Dad wore buttons:

REAGAN '80

LET'S

MAKE

AMERICA

GREAT AGAIN

I was ten then.
I believed him.
We all believed him.

One year later
August 1981:
ZAP!

What about the people
who threw eggs at our strike
cheered Ronnie Raygun
not the union?

After we lost, Uncle Russell said,
Joey, if they can't have something good
they don't want anyone else to
have something good.

I don't want to be that way.
I want to disturb this unfair universe.
And if a song can do it

I want to write that song.

ATAQUE DE NERVIOS

Tía Rosa says
my mother's heart is too small
for all her feelings

Mami loves too hard,
worries too much, and rages
at this unjust world

emotions her heart
can't hold flow into her mind
and disturb her soul

people call it an
ataque de nervios
a nervous attack

Tía Rosa tries
to pray them away but God
isn't listening

no holy water
can soothe Mami's nerves or drown
out the loud voices

only Mami hears
she's alone in this nightmare
I can't wake her up

how do I protect
her from spies only she sees?
I'd do anything

to help my mother
I gotta find a way to
stop these attacks and

keep us together
as a family before
social services

finds out that Mami
sometimes gets confused about
the past and present

can't hold down a job
'cause some days she can't even
get up outta bed

sometimes Mami acts
just like her old self but those
days don't come often

the attacks are worse
now and I don't know how long
I can hide the truth

I'm no scientist
just a kid who needs a cure
'cause love isn't enough

NOT ME . . . THIS TIME

I

I shouldn't follow Pi
half a block behind
so he won't see me.

If I don't belong at school
I sure don't belong
in his neighborhood.

I'm only going to the subway
that gets me out
of here.

II

On my way
a crowd
swallows Pi

Fight!
Fight!
Fight!

Lynbrook   or   Brooklyn
the words   the same

My heart thumps.
My hands flutter.

I'm not in the middle
not me   this time
looking out
at stone-cold faces.

At the edge of the crowd
                                this time
I watch
                    Pi

spidery arms waving
feet dancing
dodging
a light-skinned kid
almost as white as me
with thick arms
                    fists
                    that pop Pi
                    again
                    again

and I expect Pi
to crumple
or cry   like me

from the pain
the shame   but . . .

FIRST FIGHT

before the first blow finds my face I call over my shoulder JIMMY TAKE
PILAR HOME/then blood fills my mouth/sour as a penny under my
tongue/I throw down my book bag and put my fists up just like Mr.
Ashrawi taught me/I remember not to freeze/let my feet dance across
the pavement though my knees are weak/I weave when I can but like
magnets Junior's fists keep finding my flesh/hard as hammers at the
end of his jabbing arms/in the hall at school his words are sharp as
darts dipped in poison/but when it comes to disses I can give as good
as I get/Junior ain't the sharpest tool in the shed as Tito would say and
I used that to my advantage/had to 'cause even the kids who are Black
like me line up behind Junior as if standing in his shadow will hide their
own dark skin/full lips/and pelo malo/then Junior started talking about
my mother/loca/so I went after his/junkie/and maybe that's why he
decided to switch from insults swapped at school to a bloody brawl out
in the street/if Ricky were still here he'd have my back/but Ricky ain't
here/Oscar's got baseball practice and Manny's probably blowing all his
quarters playing Pac-Man over at the arcade/so today it's just me picking
Pilar up from school/and Jimmy tagging along because even though he
lives on the other side of Los Sures there aren't enough hours in the
school day for Jimmy to spend with Pilar/they're just kids but Jimmy's
big for his size and he got left back more than once/so kids pick on
him too/that's the deal/you can't be too smart/too dumb/too small/or
too big/but Mami didn't raise us like that/so Pilar made Jimmy her best
friend and the other kids soon followed her lead and learned to leave
him alone/Junior's next blow busts my lip open and spins me around
so I can see my little sister hugging the lamppost/refusing to leave me
bleeding in the street/and Jimmy looks like he's about to cry too because
he can't peel Pilar's skinny strong arms off the pole without hurting
her/but Jimmy knows that seeing me get beat to a pulp probably hurts
Pilar even more/I swipe at the blood gushing from my nose and try to
hit more than air/then over the taunts/jeers/cheers and laughter of the

kids swarming around us like bees/I hear a familiar voice/see the flash of sequins and the bounce of platinum curls as Miss Tina comes storming up the block in her strappy silver stilettos/swatting kids aside with her pocketbook so she can grab the collar of Junior's jean jacket and haul him offa me/I jump up and sock Junior hard in the stomach/low blow/I know/but I may never get the chance again since Miss Tina snatches my collar too and holds us apart/two boys dangling at the ends of her long thin arms/the gold bangles circling her wrists jangling like bells in my ears/Mami always said Miss Tina was a lady and we should treat her that way but right now she's cursing a mile a minute in English and Spanish/calling both of us a disgrace/then Junior swipes at Miss Tina instead of me/he lets fly that slur Mami told us never to say/I don't know why but that one word stings even more than loca/so I wrench myself free and smash my fist in his face/I hit Junior so hard he goes down dazed and doesn't get up right away/the crowd goes wild/even his boys sneer behind their hands and pat me on the back/then Miss Tina snares me once more and drags me off/cursing about the fingernail we made her break/I manage to yell over my shoulder GO HOME PILAR/this time my little sister listens/puts her hand inside Jimmy's/wipes her eyes with the other/and smiles with pride because her big brother just won his/first fight

NOT ME . . . THIS TIME (CONTINUED)

BOOM!
a single
drumbeat
drops
the kid
to the
pavement.

I cheer with the rest of them.
Even though Pi isn't my friend
just a kid from my class
who knows all the answers
it feels like my side won
                    for once.

TITO SAYS

that ain't like you, Pie
taps his finger against my temple
and I wince not so much from pain but
more the shame of disappointing him
you too smart to let some knucklehead
get under your skin

Tito's trying to be gentle
wiping the blood from my face
as I hold a pack of frozen peas over my left eye
he disrespected Miss Tina I mumble with my fat lip
Tito glances her way but she doesn't even look at us
her wig hangs lifeless from a Styrofoam head
on the dresser and there's a big hole in the
fishnet stockings covering her long, crossed legs
Miss Tina just grunts and says
I've heard a lot worse, baby
her short dark hair makes her look softer somehow
ruby lips puckered as she blows dry the fresh coat
of red polish on her replacement press-on nail

Tito says
you right to stand up for a lady
ain't nobody gonna protect our
women if we don't and then
I feel bad for what I said about
Junior's mom but he went
after mine first

loca
that one word lit a fire inside of me
and suddenly I wasn't Pie the straight
A student with proper home training
I was Pie the fire-breathing dragon
Junior (and his mother) didn't stand a chance
no wonder he wanted to beat
the crap outta me

I don't say any of this out loud but
it's like Tito can read my mind
never understood why, he says,
we go to war with fellas who
could be our brothers
we look so much alike
got so much in common yet
can't find a way to get along
I mean, damn—we supposed
to be on the same team
right?

I want to tell Tito how Junior
calls my mother crazy and then
disrespects my father too by
calling me
spear chucker
African booty scratcher
banana breath
monkey
cannibal

Tito says
a man's got to stand up for himself
but take a minute to understand
your opponent—figure out
what makes him tick
Junior—ain't that
Lissette's boy?

Miss Tina grunts instead
of saying yes and Tito
sits back to examine
my battered face

you know his mami's sick too, right?

the frozen peas are starting to melt
and I don't know if Tito can see
the tears spilling from my other
eye but he grips my shoulder
gives it a squeeze and doesn't
let go for a long time

then Miss Tina uncrosses her legs
and says *I could murder an egg roll*
Tito laughs and I smile too even
though my whole face hurts
at home we don't have supper
till six o'clock (sometimes later if
I'm the one cooking) it's only four now
but we still order in and sit around
the table like a regular family

Miss Tina shows me how to use
chopsticks and after we're done
Tito packs up the leftovers
for me to take home
before I go we crack
open our cookies and
read our fortunes
out loud

Miss Tina will soon meet a mysterious stranger
an exciting opportunity is heading Tito's way
mine says

THE BEST WAY TO GET RID OF AN
ENEMY IS TO MAKE A FRIEND.

FREE RIDER

My student transit pass
takes me anywhere
in this city
for
          free.

Flash it quick at the token clerk
Push through the metal gate

     clang!

skip
     down
          stairs
               in time
                    for the

     rumble, rumble
          RUMBLE!

whoosh
     of cool musty breeze
flash of   headlights

     WOW!

What is this color explosion?
Bursting to life
on the side of cars

like a dozen comic book pages
flipping past

          and

          screeeeech!

scree—
      fingers pressed in ears

                —eeching

                to
                a
                stop.

No time to make out
          shapes
          colors
          puffy
          boxy
          letters

in the salty, sweaty
shove of people
toward wide-open double doors
              don't touch me!

"Stand clear of the
closing doors . . ."
says the conductor

ding dong

whirr

thump

clack . . . clack . . clack clack
clackclackclack
clackclicketyclack

jerk forward . . .
                                    back . . .
train careening
neck snapping
smell of dirty dishwater

                                    don't stumble into me!

Squeeee-al beneath my sneakers' rubber soles
walls covered in strange signs
like symbols scratched
into stone of caves
or black-markered hieroglyphics
that make me think of
pharaohs' time.

Finally a seat
take my Walkman from my gym bag
slip headphones over my ears
I'm in the dark-tunnel punk-rock club
of my mind
clackclackclicketyclack
of the drums
thumpthump
of the bass guitar
screeeeech
of lead guitar
                                    echoing
rumblerumblerumble
Joe Strummer's rhythm guitar

working for the Clampdown!

Shoot from the tunnel

                          into daylight.

Sunbeams sparkle on the river
                          far
                          below
                          this
                          bridge

and I fly
calm at last
for the afternoon

                          free.

DEVOTION

everything
worth having
has a price

even God
expects to get
something in return
for miracles

I light a candle
when I go to mass
and cross myself
before kneeling
to recite the
Lord's Prayer

but real devotion
looks like Tía Rosa who
keeps a rosary in her purse
and probably says a hundred
Hail Marys a day
even while she's
waiting for
the bus

Marta has
a small table
in her apartment
that she covers with
a white cloth

Marta places
offerings on her altar—

        a peacock feather
        a pearl necklace
        a conch shell
        and a tiny blue
        bottle of perfume

above the table
there's a painting of a
beautiful Black mermaid
rising out of the sea
with a machete
in her hand

back on dry
land Benita's father
stands on a milk crate
and preaches on the
corner right in front
of Sal's bodega

he's fishing for
lost souls but mostly
seems to catch
true believers

they stand
enthralled
hands raised
eyes closed
swaying slightly
shouting
ALELUYA!
when you
least expect it

with her sisters
Benita hands out
leaflets that say
JESUS SAVES
across the top
I take one
and then walk
around the block
just so I can pass her again
ask for another leaflet
and watch her smile
as she says

                    Join us on Sunday.
                    All are welcome.

I don't know
what it's like
to be filled with
the Holy Spirit
to roll on the floor and
speak in tongues

I only know
that when Benita
smiles at me
my tongue twists
itself into a knot

I am
wordless
lost at sea
wishing I had
an offering
of my own
to lay at
her feet

A SORT OF TALK WITH BABCIA

"Why we no see your siostra?"
        Babcia says
and I can't answer
in a way she'd understand

because I don't speak Polish

because I don't know why
                        either.

I dribble an invisible basketball
though it might still be
field hockey season
eating up her Saturdays

and on Sundays, church.

Here an all-day thing
in not one
            but two
        foreign languages
                    Polish and Latin.

She no longer comes in for the day
the way we all used to do
                    Alina-and-me
sticking to each other
like my itchy suit
sticks to sweaty skin
        that doesn't want
        to be touched.

"You . . . go
to . . . her."

Babcia reaches into
her worn cloth purse
hands me a five-dollar bill.

    "Pociąg."

I flip through my dictionary
point to the word:
pociąg : train

She nods, and a smile
spreads across her wrinkly
full-moon face

because the moon watches us on Earth
        and knows
        everything.

Even though I'm not a hugger
        I hug her
                        with
                        both hands
        and my
        whole body too.

MS. K

when Ms. K sees my bruised face
she presses her lips together
pushes her long brown waves
behind her shoulders but she
doesn't say a word during class
afterward she calls me up to her desk
hands me a blue sheet of paper and tells me
she wants to talk to my mother
I tell her Mami works late and can't make it
to parent-teacher night but Ms. K just says
I can come in early tomorrow morning—
would that work?
I look down at the sheet she gave me
it's a flyer for some kind of art camp
not out in the woods upstate in the summer
but after school at the BK Museum
it sounds cool and all but if I can't get Mami
out of bed how am I gonna
get her to come to my school?
Ms. K sees me frowning and puts her hand
over mine for just a second
you're not in any trouble, Pierre
this is a good opportunity for
someone like you

on the way home
I think about what
someone like me means

> a poor Black kid
> from a broken home
> in the 'hood

who's going
nowhere
fast

I know Ms. K means well
but I'm nobody's charity case
then I take a closer look at the flyer
and realize this art camp costs
a hundred bucks which means
I definitely can't go so I trash
the flyer and my art dreams
as soon as I get home
but when I wake up
the next day Mami's already
in the kitchen making breakfast
in the clothes she bought when
she got that secretary job downtown
last year before the voices started
and she hid out in her bedroom or
wandered down the block in her
chancletas and robe
this morning Mami's like her old self again
Pilar beams at me as she
scarfs down her crema de maiz
I only get a few spoonfuls of mine
before Mami hustles us out the door
and tells me to walk Pilar to her school
before meeting her at mine

by the time I get there my heart
is racing even though I walked
as slowly as I could
Mami and Ms. K are sitting in the art room
laughing over cups of coffee like
they've been friends forever
Ms. K grabs her cane and stands up

she's not much bigger than me
but I feel small and foolish
standing there between
my mother and my favorite teacher
your son is one of the most talented students
I've ever had the honor to teach
I know he'd benefit greatly from
an enrichment program like this
Mami cups my face in her palm
her eyes shining with tears
and for a moment I panic
thinking she's about to come undone
but Mami just blinks away her tears
and says *I'm sure we can make it work*
I don't see how when you gotta *be* rich to
afford this kind of camp but for now I
just smile and wonder how long Mami
will be normal again

out in the hall where Ms. K can't hear
I ask Mami if she's feeling okay
wish me luck she says
with a shrug and a smile
what for? I ask
you need to be in this program, Pierre,
but I don't have that kind of money
it's okay, Mami, I tell her
but my mother's blue eyes flash at me
no, Pierre, it's not
but it will be
with a little
luck

WHITEBOY

Puerto Ricans comes in all shapes
sizes and colors—look at me and Pilar
—we look nothing alike but we're still family
I can always tell when somebody's just
real light and somebody else is white
there's something about the way they
move among us, the way they talk with
their hands, push out their lips, or laugh
with their eyes instead of opening their mouth
all it takes is a nod and I know who's one of us
and who's not

there's a new kid in my class—
Whiteboy
nerdy
quiet
keeps to himself

not saying I'm Mr. Popular but
I ain't in the market for any more friends
Manny and Oz are goofballs but they're good enough for me
and I'm still working up the nerve to talk to Benita
I got too much to deal with at home
to take on a special project at school
but something 'bout the way that Whiteboy
looked that day in the cafeteria made
me talk to him after class today

White kids stand out around here and
the few at my school tend to stick together
some try to cross over by wearing our clothes,
eating our food, listening to our music, or

sprinkling our words in their speech to add a little sazón
others take pride in standing out, not blending in
this kid—he just floats through the hall like a ghost
he's invisible almost and that keeps him safe most of the time
but at lunch last week he was eating by himself
not bothering nobody and this beefy dude with carrot-colored
hair walked by and flipped over his tray
the kid grabbed his Walkman so it didn't get soaked with milk
and then cleaned up the mess as the beefy dude
sneered from his seat across the aisle

I got my own jerks to deal with
so I didn't do nothing then but today
I stopped by his desk just to say hey
nothing real chummy but I let him know
that some of us eat with Ms. K in the art room
if you clean a few paintbrushes or sweep the floor
she'll let you sit at one of the wide tables so
you can eat your lunch in peace
do your homework
read a book
be yourself

Is that where you eat?
he asked and I nodded
before moving on
called over my shoulder
Tuesdays & Thursdays
then Manny saw me in the hall
pulled the headphones off his ears
and planted them on mine so
I could groove to the smooth
flow of Grandmaster Flash
it's like a jungle sometimes
it makes me wonder
how I keep from going under

ONLY SILENCE HERE

I

No crowds at this Long Island station
        touching me
pushing me forward

only Alina's letter to me
after I wrote her
about honors class
Pi
murals I gaped at
on subway cars and buildings
Mom and Dad arguing
about me in public school
with too many kids
                with those *kids.*

I memorized her answer
I'm busy with school.
My team's in the finals this weekend
but when it's over
let's meet   sometime
                    somewhere
                    in the middle

and Babcia's words:

You . . . go
to . . . her.

No one walks alongside me
     on the sidewalk
     or the street

telling me
I don't belong
             here
             anymore.

Still, I'm a tourist
a stranger
on streets
I once walked
rode my bike
or passed on the school bus.

Lynbrook is not my home.
Hewlett is not the town where
     I go to school.

But did I ever really belong
if I could fade away
so quickly?

A house
       a family
             erased
             just
             like
             that?

II

On Long Island
fall Saturdays mean yard work

clipped grass and raked leaves
surrounding tidy homes.

A leaf blower's roar
avoids conversation.

Rolled-up car windows
hush the music.

I've grown accustomed to music

blasting from windows
        boom boxes
        cars

the tug of war of   rhythms
                  melodies
                  words
        from all directions

languages

        spoken
        sung
        carried on drumbeats
                chords
        break-danced on sidewalks
        painted on walls.

Only silence
            here.

III

I don't expect surprises

especially not music
bleeding from the maintenance shed
between the all girls' high school
and my old lower school

> lured to that same wood-slat shed
> and beaten up inside,
> once in fourth grade
> again last year
> in sixth grade

Now music lures me
Patti Smith   punk goddess
        screaming
G-L-O-R-I-A . . . Gloria!
to the straight-up beat
of drum
          keyboard
                    guitar

That's my sister's favorite song!
She opened my ears
                    my mind
Alina
      my own   punk goddess

Could she be there
                    warming up
                    for the big game
                    in her own way?

I follow the music
push open the door
what I see
                    more shocking
than five bullies staring back at me.

Alina on the beat-up sofa
      music pounding
Claire on the same beat-up sofa
      Patti Smith wailing
girls in matching
blue-and-white uniforms
                          kissing . . .
My throat   quivers
                closes.

I press my back to the wall
as if I could disappear through it
and make what I saw disappear
through the wall
of my skull.

Music clicks off.

"JJ, what are you doing here?"

Words pinball in my belly—

Babcia gave me money
so I could see you.
Then you wrote me your team
made the championship game—

they churn into sputters
as Alina says,
"Look, I can explain . . ."

and my fingers go numb.

Alina Claire
two girls kissing
on the mouth

kissing . . .

Do   these   things
      really   happen
in   this   world?

BRIBE

"You can't tell anyone, JJ."

It's only a kiss
            between best friends.
Nothing more.

Claire laughs
            a short, harsh laugh.

"Look at his eyes and mouth. Like
cute big buttons," she says.

"Just shut up, Claire."

Alina stands
straightens her uniform
smooths out imaginary wrinkles.

"I need to figure this out."

She pops open the cassette player
side closest to her
yanks out Patti Smith
drops the tape into her gym bag
hands me the boom box.

"Here. Take it. It only gets me
in trouble."

I cradle it in my arms
dual cassette players

to make mixtapes
like the ones she made for me
when she introduced me to

                              Punk
                              Ska
                              Reggae

taught me
                    to embrace the
          backbeat
out of step with the other kids.

Was she out of step all along
          backbeat
                         in her own way?

Is this why my parents
          never say
          her name?

"You don't have to bribe me.
I can keep a secret."
I hold out the boom box.

Alina crosses her arms
against her chest
not reaching for it

and
Claire nods
                as if to say
You'd better.

BASKY YEAH

I ask Ms. K to teach me how to say his name
it's French like mine but he's got
a lot more syllables

     here's how it looks: JEAN-MICHEL BASQUIAT

     here's how it sounds: JAWN ME SHELL BASKY YEAH

I call him JMB for short
though he's SAMO© on the street
sometimes Ms. K brings in her art magazines
and lets me flip through them during lunch
they're heavy and glossy and cost a lot
so I make sure to eat my crinkle-cut fries
and wipe all the ketchup off my fingers
before I start to turn the pages

I don't have to look up to know
Ms. K is watching me
I wonder, is this a test?
if so what do I have to prove—
that someone like me could
become someone like him?
is this camp part of an experiment
it ain't charity 'cause thanks to Tía Rosa
Mami paid the fee in full
you got every right to be there, mijo
that's what Mami said
so you walk in there with your head held high
I gotta go to church with my aunt from now on

but I guess that's a small price to pay
I'd rather go to the Pentecostal church
where Benita's father could see what
an upstanding young man I am but
at mass I can still say her name just
like I do each night when I kneel
to count my blessings

I turn the page and try to focus
on JMB instead of Benita
I want to tell Ms. K that I like his style
but *like* isn't really the right word
can I say that JMB seems really pissed off?
I look at the paintings he's made and
all I see is chaos
colors words
crowns skulls
it's like he's got X-ray vision and wants
everybody else to have it too
I don't know if I could be that brave
open my brain my heart my guts
and let it spill all over the place
but folks are paying beaucoup bucks
for JMB's stuff so it's gotta be
more than a mess—there's a
message he's trying to send

Ms. K must get tired of watching me
'cause I hear the scrape of her chair
and then she grabs her cane off the
edge of her desk and comes over to
stand behind me
what do you see? she asks
simple question, right?
I got this

I like how he paints all over everything
I tell her pointing to a couple of wooden doors
with the knobs still attached
it's like he went through the empty lot
next to my building and claimed
all the stuff nobody wants
and turned it into art
Ms. K nods and says *objet trouvé*
she says it again more slowly
obb-jeh true vay
and I ask her to spell it so I
can write it down
it's French for "found object"
she tells me, pulling my pen from my
fingers so she can add an
accent to the last *e*
what else do you see, Pierre?
I look down at the page in front of me
and decide to tell Ms. K half the truth
he paints us . . . or himself black—
REAL BLACK—like he's proud of who he
is even if it scares other folks
he's a king and there's his crown but
then look here he writes
MOST ~~YOUNG~~
KINGS GET
THIER HEAD█ CUT OFF

he makes mistakes and fixes them himself
or just leaves them out there
that's pretty cool it's like he's showing
us he's not perfect he's
still figuring it all out

I don't tell Ms. K that I also like how
JMB paints cops pink as pigs with vampire fangs
but she points to that painting anyway and

tells me that the black figure in between
the pig cops with their batons raised over
their ugly heads is Michael Stewart
a friend of JMB who got caught tagging
an LL train on the Lower East Side
when they brought him to Bellevue
Hospital he was hog-tied and unconscious
do you know what that means? Ms. K asks
I look at the wobbly black halo JMB drew
around his friend's head and I feel dragon Pie
stirring inside so I don't open my mouth I just
nod and then the bell rings so I close the
magazine and hand it back to Ms. K but
she tells me to keep it I don't know if
she means for good or just for now
but I put it in my bag and study every
page as I ride the LL train into the city
after school and catch the 2/3 back into
Brooklyn I think about Michael Stewart
and all the times I've scratched my tag
on a park bench or the bus window and I
wonder who will paint a halo around my
head if the cops do the same thing to me
then the train pulls into the station
Eastern Parkway/Brooklyn Museum and
I put the magazine back in my bag ready
to make Mami and Tía Rosa and Ms. K
proud

SEEDS

Tito gives me a couple bucks to help out in the garden
it's for the community but hardly anyone shows up
at least not when there's work to be done
for Tito it's a labor of love
he talks to his flowers like they're family
and even says sorry before snipping each stem
I show up 'cause I need the money but also
for the way Mami smiles when I bring her a rose
sometimes I dream about being here with Benita
we could sit on the bench Tito pulled outta the
back seat of a Pinto and let the scent of hibiscus
turn the smelly East River into the Caribbean Sea
in my dream Benita doesn't laugh when I tell her
I don't really hate my deadbeat dad
that deep down I hope he's thinking 'bout me
the same way I'm almost always thinking 'bout him

I was born in this city of concrete and steel but
when I work in Tito's garden feel my knees sinking
into the soil dig with my bare hands till there's dirt
under every nail I think about my abuelo and his
father before him all our ancestors coaxing life
from the ground not 'cause they have to but 'cause
they know that when you're gentle with the earth it
will share its secrets and its beauty and its bounty with you
when Tito talks about the garden like that I feel like I'm listening
to Socrates or some monk from the Middle Ages he says
youngbloods out here in these streets think power comes
from a blade or a bullet but I'm telling you, Pie, ain't no
force stronger than life and that's what I'm giving you

I hold out my hand and Tito drops seeds so light
I can barely feel the weight of them in my palm
I close my fingers around them to stop the wind
from blowing them away but Tito peels my fingers
back and says *Don't shut the wind out, Pie.*
El viento is like la mano de Dios.
Mami taught us to say grace before eating and to
pray before we go to bed, but I haven't spent a whole
lotta time thinking 'bout God—why would I
with my family as messed up as it is?
but maybe Tito's right—maybe it is the hand of God
that scatters seeds and people all over the world
maybe that's why Mami left her island and came to America
left Los Sures to attend college in the city at the same time
my father arrived from across the sea
maybe I wasn't an accident after all

ART ROOM

I

At lunch Tuesday
three days
                    after I said goodbye
      to Alina
                    and hello
      to a dual-cassette boom box

I stand in a corner
            by the
            cafeteria
            door
brown bag with peanut butter sandwich
in one hand
milk carton in the other   trying to decide.

Last week
            after Jack-O'-Lantern white boy
            tipped over my tray
that genius kid Pi
invited me to the art room
                        wherever it is.

He said I could eat my lunch in peace
like it was something he needed to do
                        hide
but I've seen him with friends

                  and I wonder
                  if it's another trick

a setup
like the maintenance shed
at my old school
of taunts
and fists
and my sister kissing Claire.

"Yo, move it!"

No one else sitting
at my usual corner of the table
closest to cash register and lunch aides.

"You're standing in the door, pendejo!"

Pumpkin Head's   across the room
maybe messing   with someone else.

He'll be back

and the noise still drowns out my music

and yesterday in social studies
Mr. Zullo said,

> *Along with the Founding Fathers*
> *this honors class*
> *will do a report on leaders*
> *and leadership.*
> *One-third*
> *of your final*
> *   unit*
> *   grade.*

"Out of my way, loser!"

I don't belong in that class   this school
but if Pi eats lunch
                in the art room
maybe he can help me
because he likes to get the answers right
and explain to kids
                who
                don't
                understand.

        And maybe he'll even
        like me.

I slip out the door
into the main office
wait for the secretary to notice me
                        as my milk carton
                        turns warm in my hand
                        drippy and slippery
                        from condensation.

"How can I help you, young man?"

"Can you, uh, please
point me in the direction
                of the art room?"

II

Pi's not in the art room when I get there
and three kids are finishing up.
Tall light-brown boy with wisp of a mustache
wads his paper bag
                throws it at the trash can
                                misses

Two girls
one light skin with boy-short hair
the other darker with bouncy ponytail
tilt their trays
until the leftovers
of their free or reduced lunches
fall—*thunk!*—to the metal bottom

                              free or reduced lunches
                              Mom refused to apply for
                              saying, *We don't take welfare*
                              like those people.
                              We don't beg help
                              from anyone,
                              as she crumpled up the form
                              flung it at the wastebasket
                              in Babcia's kitchen
                              missed by a mile.

Pi's right.
It's quiet in the art room.
I can hear my music.
Alone.
Safe.

SPIN

Mami says when she met Pilar's father
she thought he looked like Héctor Lavoe.

Personally I don't see the resemblance,
and Tony sure can't carry a tune, but he

spins Pilar around the living room and
tries to pull Mami into his arms as well.

I play deejay since there's nothing else
for me to do but keep the music flowing.

Tony barely looks at me—he even pays me to
leave so he can have the family he really wants.

I take his money and go to the bodega for him,
buy a pack of smokes and take back the change

even though he always tells me to keep it. Buy
something for yourself, Pedro, is what he says.

But I don't want his fake generosity when I know
deep down Tony hates me—won't even say my

name. That's how scared he is of my father's ghost.
Mami says the real reason Tony's jealous of me is

'cause Pilar told her father that I'm her best friend.
Tony put his hands on me once and that was all it

took for Mami to kick him to the curb. He still comes
around to see his precious golden-haired princess and

I know Pilar loves him even though Tony tells
corny jokes and wears too much Aqua Velva.

He treats her like a doll even though Pilar hates
wearing the frilly dresses Tony keeps on buying.

With her golden ringlets spilling down her back
Pilar looks like an angel, and people on the street

actually sigh when she walks by holding Tony's hand.
It makes him so proud but that's not the real Pilar.

She should get an Oscar for that performance!
Pilar plays that role 'cause even at eight she knows

what people want her to be. It's a racket and
Pilar knows just how to play those suckers.

She lets the viejos pat her on the head, then she takes
the quarters they press into her hand and we go to

the arcade with our mouths full of Bazooka gum
or Now and Laters for me and a Fun Dip for Pilar.

Only Mami and Jimmy know Pilar the way I do.
My little sister may not get A's in school but that

don't mean she's stupid. People get so caught up
in the color of her eyes that they don't notice how

Pilar sees *everything*. She'd make a great spy but what
she really wants to do is dance. Not ballet or salsa;

Pilar wants to bust a move like the B-boys on the street
with their shell-toe Adidas, gold chains, and tracksuits.

We went to El Puente one day 'cause Manny told us
about a show and the crew onstage was tearing it up.

One dude pressed his ear to the floor and let his legs spin
like a windmill but when he froze, his Kangol fell off his head

and a long brown braid fell into his face. Pilar gasped
and tugged my hand—*It's a girl!* After that couldn't

nobody tell Pilar she couldn't break-dance too. She still
puts on a dress and sits like a doll on Tony's lap but as

soon as he leaves, Pilar puts on her Pumas and goes to work.
I taught her what I know (which isn't much) and one night we

three watched in awe as Michael Jackson slid across the TV
like he was walking on the moon—even Mami had to admit

MJ was smooth. Pilar practices every day, hoping to convince
Mami that having a B-girl for a daughter isn't such a bad thing.

Out here you got to be ready for whatever the world throws
at you and that means having all the right moves. Mami thinks

"crew" is the same as "gang." They do battle but it's about
showing off your skillz, not hurting nobody. These days if

Mami's lost in the fog of her mind I take Pilar over to El
Puente after school and leave her there to learn from the

pros while I bag groceries to earn a little pocket money.
Manny's uncle manages the store and it's not a lot but I'd

rather bag fruit and canned goods than wind up in a body bag
working as a lookout or mule for Manny's cousin Juan. I try not

to judge—we all gotta hustle out here—and I ain't the only kid
trying to keep the lights on and put food on the table. But Mami's

counting on me to keep the family together and that means
knowing when to roll the dice and when to play it safe.

KOŁACZKI

want one?

powdered sugar   rings Whiteboy's mouth

his head's turned my way   but his eyes don't meet mine

they're locked on the   wide sea   of desk between us

the half-eaten cookie in his left   hand is about to spill   its red guts

so I nod   take the other one   off the piece of foil he slides my way

co-watch-key   he mumbles with his

mouth full of   sweetness

for a minute we chew   in silence

I make sure not to   spill   the sweet apricot filling in the center

of my cookie onto   the glossy pages of Ms. K's art magazine

He picks up his pen   goes back to making angry birds in his notebook

I steal another glance and   realize what I thought were wings

are actually

notes

you   write music?

Whiteboy nods   and the rims of his ears   turn red

around the black   foam of his headphones

I wonder why   there's no pride in

the line of his mouth   the tilt of his head

I don't know any other   composers our age but Whiteboy's lips roll in

his chin goes down   like he's waiting for a fist   in the gut

bracing himself for   the lash of

cruel laughter

so I ask   *who'd you choose for   your social studies project?*

and Whiteboy dares to look   at me then   even cracks a smile

before saying a name   I've never   heard before

it sounds foreign   like his cookies   and I can tell

by the pride   in his eyes that this dude

must be important   to him   the same way

my choice   Lumumba   is important

to me

LIKE ME, PLEASE

I

In the art room on Thursday
      because I show up on time
               and he shows up
I ask Pi if he likes music.
He grins.
      "Yeah."

"What kind?"

"Everything.
      Except country.
      It's whack. Sorry,
          Whiteboy."

"S'okay. I don't like country either.
I'm into punk, like the Clash.
I'm learning to play guitar.
And you?"

Pi taps his book bag.
It makes a metallic sound
like a miniature
      steel drum.

"This."

Through an
      unzipped   gap

I
spot a
single spray
c a n   t o s s e d
h a p h a z a r d l y
i n t o   s h a d o w
o f   s k e t c h p a d,
colored pencils,
m a r k e r s, like a
kaleidoscope of
colors and shapes

Does Pi paint comic-book panels
        on subway cars?
Or giant glistening murals
        on sides of buildings?
Do I gape at his work
        through windows
        of trains pushing
                into the light?

II

Minutes later
when I'm wiping down Ms. Kirschbaum's tables

I realize
I talked to Pi

more than a few words
                a real-life conversation
and

he didn't make fun of me.

ART CAMP (HAIKU)

the museum is
open to the public but
closed to kids like me

security guard
wants to look inside *my* bag
but everyone else

gets to glide on by
'cause the museum was made
for rich kids like them

white kids don't have to
prove they belong in rooms full
of gold-framed paintings

even the African
gallery is made for them
those masks behind glass

can't tell the story
of how they were stolen from
the folks who made them

for sacred reasons
not to inspire white artists
who can't come up with

an original
concept 'cause their own culture
been dying for years

so just like vampires
they suck life from our music
our art, our language

and now here I am
in a room in the basement
with kids I don't know

who must wonder why
someone like me has his hand
in the air again

let me tell you why:
I got a right to be here
my voice matters too

I came here to learn
and if you give me a chance
I might surprise you

LOST & FOUND

technically this
JESUS SAVES leaflet
is not an objet trouvé
since Benita handed it
to me (twice) but there
were plenty more blowing
down the street and
crumpled up in the
wire trash bin on
the corner so I
figure it still
counts

Ms. K told me
to look for patterns
in JMB's paintings
except the word
she used first
was *motif*

what symbols or
words show up again
and again in his work?
ask yourself *why*
Pierre

repetition has
meaning when
it's deliberate
that's what I've
learned in art camp

so far so I try to
be deliberate
too

what means
the most to me?
family always
comes first

        then
        my culture
        my friends
        my girl
        my 'hood
        my future
        my dreams

MIXTAPE #1

At home I make Pi a mixtape.

	All my favorite			
C		that fit on		s
L	t		s	o
A	w o		i d	n
S	2		es	g
H	thirty-minute			s

The next day
in first-period science
I hand him the tape
test my hypothesis:
if I give Pi a gift
then he will become
                my friend.

Wait until last period
social studies
when Mr. Zullo
has us work in pairs.

"I listened to your tape
at lunch. It's okay,"
Pi says.

"Only okay?"

                        Words catch in my throat.

"No, it's good. I liked it.

Have you ever heard Afrika Bambaataa?"

"No."

I reach for my pencil
flip to a fresh notebook page
ask him to spell out the name.

"Got some more for you.
Cold Crush Brothers.
Lovebug Starski.
Grandmaster Flash."

"I heard of Grandmaster Flash."

Silently, I thank Alina
because without her
I'd have no chance
with this friend.

"Cool, uh . . ."

He stops
stares at me.
I glance to the side.

He doesn't know my name.

"I'm JJ."

"Yeah, thanks, JJ." He taps
the label. "One thing, though.
I spell Pie with an *e* at the end
like apple or cherry
or American
        pie."

"Don McLean, 1971," I say
                on auto-
                play.

"Who's that?"

"He wrote that song called 'American Pie.'
My dad used to like it a lot."

I don't tell Pie
Dad stopped
playing his fancy stereo
after the strike
and sold it soon after
as if that was
                for him
the day
the music
died.

Pie doesn't say anything either.

I change the subject.

"My favorite songs
are the ones
with the backbeat
like in reggae
                the guitar chord
a half step behind
        the drumbeat."

I slap the desk
                and tap my foot
        on the floor
                right after.

"Pankowski! Stop fooling around.
You're the last one
I thought
I'd have to call out."

"Sorry, sir. We're working together."

I turn to Pie
with an *e* at the end.

"So who's the leader that you picked?"

CLASH MIXTAPE
FOR PIE

Side One	Side Two
"Career Opportunities"	"The Magnificent Seven"
"Police & Thieves"	"Somebody Got Murdered"
"London Calling"	"One More Time"
"Rudie Can't Fail"	"One More Dub"
"Clampdown"	"Police on My Back"
"The Guns of Brixton"	"The Call Up"
"Revolution Rock"	"Should I Stay or Should I Go"
"Train in Vain"	"Lost in the Supermarket"

EXTRA CREDIT

even countries
have fathers
so why not
me?

why don't
we study the
nation's founding
mothers?

they're the
ones who hold
life inside

and make
a world in
the womb

plus

mothers are
the ones
who stay

HALLOWEEN

Tony bought Pilar a stuffed E.T.
it's half as tall as she is so Pilar decided
she's going trick-or-treating as Gertie
it's not much of a stretch for her to play
a cute little sister with blond pigtails

Oz thinks he can still fit into the blue tights
he wore last year when he went as Superman
Oz won't have any trouble parting his straight
black hair on the side and with just a dab of gel
he can add Superman's signature curl

me?
I'm leaving Cloud City to bring
Lando Calrissian down to Los Sures
Marta promises her hot comb will
give me waves like Billy Dee Williams
I'll make a slick mustache with my Sharpie and
Mami's blue rain poncho will work as my cape
Manny's going as Indiana Jones so he offered to
lend me his glow-in-the-dark lightsaber but
Lando's a smuggler—not a Jedi like Luke
—so I gotta find a ray gun instead

I thought JJ might wanna come with us
lose the glasses, add a black vest and he
could pass for Han Solo but JJ says they don't
really do Halloween in his home—they celebrate
All Saints' Day instead and he promised his grandmother
he'd go to the cemetery with her to lay flowers
on his grandfather's grave

probably for the best—Manny and Oz
wouldn't care if JJ came along and it's not like
he talks a whole lot but some things just don't
go together if you know what I mean

You know Lando's a traitor
Manny says and I guess that's true
but it's not like I got a whole lotta options
I don't see too many brothers saving the
universe up on the silver screen

Oz wants to lug around a broken brick all night just
so he can fake splitting it in half with Superman's laser vision
I don't wanna haul nothing but a pillowcase full of candy
but I'll humor him and play along 'cause this is one night
when anything goes—you can be anyone on Halloween
pretend you got special powers knowing full well that
the next day you'll go back to being an ordinary kid
who hungers for heroes that Hollywood won't create

Leader Worksheet

Social Studies 7H-8   Mr. Zullo
JJ Pankowski   October 25, 1982

Your chosen leader: Lech Wałęsa

Place and Date of Birth: Popowo, Poland, September 29, 1943

Place and Date of Death: still alive

Key moments in life that shaped your leader's character:
1961: finished high school and worked as electrician
1967: started work at Lenin Shipyard in Gdańsk, Poland
1969: got married
1976: fired from Lenin Shipyard and put in jail
1980: started Solidarity union and sneaked into the shipyard by
climbing a fence to lead a strike
1982: government broke strike and put Lech back in jail

How did this person create change in their community, country,
or world?
He founded the union Solidarność, which means Solidarity, and led
the strike that made it Poland's first free union.

In what way is this person similar to the Founding Fathers, and
in what way is this person different?
He's similar in that he wanted his people to be free. He's different
in that he's in Poland and speaks Polish rather than English.

In what way has this person inspired you?

If you could ask this person three questions, what would they be?

DIG DEEPER

I

Pie slides his finger
diagonally
  across
    my
     worksheet.

"I think you should
    dig
    deeper
    here
where you say the only difference
between Lech Wałęsa   and the Founding Fathers
is that he speaks Polish."

He pronounces the name
   Letch Wall-ey-ssa

and I tell him, "That's not how
you say it. It's *Lekh Vahl-when-za*.
    Like influenza."

And he says, "That's
    not
    my
    point."

II

Like everyone else
Pie thinks
I can't do the work.

Pie's different.
He's trying to help me
with this work.

III

I lay my head
on folded arms
so close to the art room table
I smell
paint
turpentine
and perfume
        from the girl
        who must have sat here
        before me.

"My bad, JJ.
Don't wanna disrespect
                his name

and your facts are interesting . . ."
                        the ones I copied from
                        the encyclopedia
                        except for the last fact
                        which happened this year
                        and which Dad and Uncle Russell
                        talked about on Sunday after church
                        over a bottle of vodka
                        and a twelve-pack of beer

"I liked the part
where he climbed the fence

to lead the workers on strike
after the shipyard fired him."

"Not the shipyard. The government
fired him," I say.
"The Communist government."

                    Though it wasn't
                    a Communist government
                    that fired my father
                            and Uncle Russell
                    and took our old lives
                                    away
                    but the president who said
                    Communists are the enemy
                    we're not like them
                    and we stand up to them.

IV

I take my worksheet from Pie
cross out my answers to the question:

*In what way is this person similar to the Founding Fathers, and in what
way is this person different?*

I imagine
two aunts
and an uncle
I've never met
in a country I've never seen
in a city, Warsaw
invaded by one side   then another
flattened by bombs and big guns.

                    The encyclopedia
                    had pictures from the war

                              even if my grandparents
                              didn't.

One aunt
crushed in a bombing.

Another aunt
married in Poland and happy.

                              At least that's what Dad says.

The uncle no one talks about
on the   other side
                              in the government
                              against Lech Wałęsa
                              against Solidarity

even though
we're supposed to be
family.

Solidarity means
we all belong
we all work together
we're like union brothers
            and sisters

but my family is broken
                  and scattered
in Poland   and   in America

                  and I'm here alone.

Loner   or   Leader

                  Time to choose.

I flip my paper
to the other side.

Lech Wałęsa is similar to the Founding Fathers because he stood up to a big country that had taken away his people's freedom, and he wasn't afraid to die or go to jail to win their independence and freedom. He's different because he was poor instead of rich and he didn't do well in school or have much education. He also believed everyone should be able to join a union and fight for their rights.

PA'LANTE

I do all I can for my mother. The food I cook tastes so good that I can
usually get her to eat but when she locks herself in her room and even

Pilar's sobs can't coax her out, then I have to call for help. Except
today our phone doesn't work 'cause Mami hasn't paid the bills in

a while. I stack them neatly on the kitchen counter but she can't see
them 'cause she only leaves her room to use the toilet in the middle

of the night when she thinks me and Pilar are asleep (I'm not). So I go
down the hall and knock on Mr. Ashrawi's door. With his oxygen tank

he can't get around all that well but he always lets me in and I always
take him a plate of food when we have extra so tonight when I need to

call for help Mr. Ashrawi lets me in right away and silently watches from
his recliner as I call my tío up in the Bronx and tell him what's going on.

When Uncle Lou shows up he's not alone. His girlfriend Marta is with him
which means me and Pilar each get a long hug and when it's my turn

I try not to cry as I press my face into her softness and breathe in her
spicy perfume. "Don't worry, papi, everything's gonna be okay," she says.

I nod without looking her in the eye and that's when I notice that
Marta has brought her cosmetics case and when Uncle Lou can't

get Mami to respond by yelling and pounding on the door with his
palm, Marta pushes him aside and starts talking softly in Spanish, her

lips close to the door. Before long we all hear the click that means Mami's ready to open up but she doesn't come out. Instead Marta

opens the door just enough to fit her curvy body inside. I manage to get a glimpse of Mami before the door closes and what I see makes

tears fill up my eyes again but I can't let Pilar see me crying so I put my arm around her shoulders, give her a squeeze, and tell her to go

get the playing cards. Pilar loves Go Fish and I know Uncle Lou don't mind playing for a while since it keeps her mind off what's happening

behind Mami's closed door. If it was just me and my tío we'd play dominoes but when Marta opens the door to Mami's room she tells

me and Lou to clear out so she can start working her magic. "The spa is now open. Pilar, chica, you want a makeover, too?" Lou nods at

the window and says, "That's our cue, kid." I follow him out onto the fire escape where he lights up and blows a stream of smoke into the

night sky. I shiver a little and ask Uncle Lou to tell me about his time with the Young Lords, the years when he wasn't much older than me,

wore a beret, and did crazy stuff like piling mounds of garbage in the middle of Third Avenue to force the sanitation department to respect the

barrio. "Those were the days, papi—we did it all: free breakfast for the kids, health care for the old folks, and education for us all so we could

free our minds." Uncle Lou stops talking and the smile on his face slowly vanishes. / *These dreams* / *These empty dreams* . . .

I know he's probably thinking about the time he spent locked up so I tell him about the worst teacher at my school, Mr. Zullo, and how

he never calls on me even when my hand is raised and he knows I
know the right answer. "Now we got this project—we have to write

about a leader who changed the world and I don't wanna write about
some dead white guy . . . even though I know that's the only way

to get an A." Uncle Lou nods and tosses his butt into the alley. "You
thinking 'bout picking one of the Young Lords for your project?

Plenty to choose from—you got Cha-Cha Jimenez who started it all
out in Chicago and then you got the Nuyoricans like Felipe Luciano

and Pablo 'Yoruba' Guzmán—and you can't forget the hermanas:
Iris Morales, Denise Oliver, and Sylvia Rivera—she started that uprising

down in the Village. You know about Stonewall, right?" Before I can
answer, Uncle Lou shakes his head and looks away. I can't tell if he's

looking at something real or something in his mind's eye. "We tried,
you know. We really tried. Who knows what we mighta done if the

Feds hadn't busted us up. Made us turn on each other—just like they
did with the Panthers. And where are we now?" Uncle Lou nods with

sad eyes at the smoldering trash and rubble in the vacant lot next to
our building. "It's a shame, man. It's a damn shame. And they

locked a whole bunch of us up but *we* know who the real criminals are.
We know." I roll my lips in and nod. Uncle Lou's been through a

lot and now he's here taking care of Mami even though he's her little
brother. I try not to call Tía Rosa 'cause she asks too many questions

and always makes us feel like this is our fault, like Mami wouldn't be
this way if Pilar and I were better kids or if we all went to mass each

week or if Mami got married and had a man to depend on. Uncle Lou doesn't judge or blame us, he just tries to help and that's why I'm not

surprised when he punches my shoulder (not hard) and tells me to spill the beans. "I can tell you got something on your mind, papi.

You worried 'bout your mom?" I nod again but say, "Actually, Tío . . . I been thinking 'bout my dad." Uncle Lou nods and waits for me to go on.

"I thought maybe . . . maybe I could write about an African leader. You told me once that he was a revolutionary." "Definitely!" Uncle Lou says,

leaning in so I can hear him over the sirens and shouting in the street. "You got plenty to choose from—Nkrumah, Kenyatta. Shoot—

you could go way back and write about Ramses. Or Taharqa—the Black pharaoh." That sounds cool but tell him I was thinking about

Patrice Lumumba. "He's from the Congo, right?" Uncle Lou's smile creeps back across his face and his eyes go soft for a few seconds.

"Your father—he ain't here and I know that's hard for you but he'd be proud of you, papi. Real proud. I know I am." Uncle Lou reaches out

and pulls me close so he can plant a kiss on my forehead. "I miss him, I guess." (Can you miss someone you never met?) "And I do wish I

could talk to my father sometimes. But I got you. I got Tito. I got Mr. Ashrawi. I'm good." "You good?" Uncle Lou asks playfully. "I'm good,"

I reply with a grin. "Then go do your homework, muchacho, and I'm gonna go down the hall and pay my respects to my friend—*if* I can

make it through Marta's 'spa' without coming out smelling like roses and covered in glitter." We both laugh, then Uncle Lou kisses the top of my head and climbs back through the window leaving me alone on the fire escape. I climb up to the roof 'cause from there I can see the

lights on the Williamsburg Bridge. It stretches across the East River to Loisaida. The East River leads out to the Atlantic Ocean. My father is

somewhere on the other side of the ocean. Maybe he has other sons in his other life. Maybe he doesn't even know I exist. I climb back down

the fire escape and slip inside our apartment. Mami looks like a movie star. She's laughing and dabbing pink lipstick on Pilar's parted lips.

I look at Marta and hope my smile tells her how grateful I am. When Mami gets better, I will ask her to give me my father's full name.

Maybe it's not too late to find him. Maybe Uncle Lou is right. Maybe my father would be proud of me.

Leader Worksheet

Social Studies 7H-8
Pierre Velez

Mr. Zullo
October 25, 1982

Your chosen leader: Patrice Lumumba

Place and Date of Birth: Katako-Kombe, Zaire; 1925

Place and Date of Death: Lubumbashi, Democratic Republic of the Congo; 1961

Key moments in life that shaped your leader's character:

How did this person create change in their community, country, or world?

In what way is this person similar to the Founding Fathers, and in what way is this person different?
—Lumumba never enslaved anybody
—Lumumba believed Black people were fully human (not 3/5)
—Lumumba wanted his country to be free & independent, not a colony that was controlled by Belgium

In what way has this person inspired you?

If you could ask this person three questions, what would they be?
Leader of the MNC (Mouvement National Congolais)
United his people
Made colonizers nervous (Belgium and USA)
Uttered the truth through passtionate poetry and speeches
Met with UN secretariat in NYC
Believed Africa was at the dawn of freedom
Assasinated at age 35

MY NEW WORLD

Manny and Oz think I'm nuts
and maybe I am
I mean how often does a cute girl
stop by my locker to ask if
I'm going to the dance on Friday?
the answer is: probably not
since Benita can't go
she'll be at church with her father
and there's no one else I want to dance with
but I can't say that out loud so I play it cool
wink and tell Ana I'll see her around
she smiles and writes her number on my hand
before walking away with her homegirls
Manny can't believe a girl that fine is into me
and the truth is, neither can I
Oz slaps me on the back like I've hit a home run
and says no doubt about it—Ana's a ten
that's what they do now, give the girls we grew up with
a number on a scale from one to ten which is why
I haven't told them how I feel about Benita
I know just what they'd say and I don't want
her name coming outta their mouths
unless they say it with respect

we been friends since forever but sometimes I
feel like Manny and Oz are a pair of shoes
that don't really fit me anymore
when I told them about the program at
the museum they just nodded and went
back to comparing their Donkey Kong scores
everything's gotta be about a number and I don't know

how to tell them about JMB and how I want to
learn to do with my hands what he does with his
how I'm combing the bloque for objet trouvé
so I can paint a masterpiece that will wipe the
smug smiles off the other kids at the museum
who only want to paint like Picasso or Monet

one Asian girl Sue took the train with me after class
she asked if I liked Andy Warhol and Keith Haring too
I didn't even know who they were but she didn't
make me feel dumb, she told me they were
white artists with rich and famous friends
who liked to party with JMB downtown
Sue also told me there's a gallery in SoHo
showing some of JMB's art
"You should totally check it out," she said
before getting off the train and I nodded
like that was something I do all the time
never been to SoHo and I know Manny
and Oz won't want to go
could I go by myself? would they let me in?
the museum is open to the public and
they gave us ID so we don't have to pay
when we show up for class

if I want to find a place for
myself in this new world
I'm gonna need
a bigger pair
of shoes

SOUP

at lunch on Thursday
I tell Ms. K about my last
class at the museum and how
Sue told me about Warhol and Haring
and their epic parties downtown
Ms. K pulls a book off the shelf behind her desk
and opens it to a painting of a can of tomato soup
how is that art? I ask and wonder if someone like me
could paint a can of Goya beans and become a star
(I doubt it) then I ask Ms. K if she knows about the
gallery in SoHo where I could see JMB's paintings
up close instead of on the pages of a magazine and
she surprises me by saying *let's go together!*
I can meet you at the gallery this Saturday—
do you know how to get there?

I'm about to shake my head when
a voice behind us says *I do*

Ms. K and I turn around at the same time
and see JJ hovering above us like a ghost
Wonderful! Ms. K exclaims—*why don't you*
meet Pierre in front of the school around noon
you two can take the train into the city and
I'll meet you there at one—that works, right?
before I can answer the bell rings and
everybody hustles to get to class
and I realize whether I like it or
not it's a done deal

JAKOŚ TO BĘDZIE*

Why did I say I knew
    how to get
    to the gallery
when I've never been to SoHo
    and it's nothing but
    a black dot
    on a green line
    on a subway map
    turning wrinkled and gray
    in my backpack?

Still, a nice teacher asked me
    to come along
    and Pie liked my mixtape
    and helped me with my project
    so he won't turn against me
    if I say the wrong thing
    or if I get him and me lost
    even though I can see
    every street a thin black line
    like a sheet-music grid
          the map
          Ms. Kirschbaum
          drew me
          from the subway
          to the gallery.
If I could take myself   all the way to Long Island
          alone

to see Alina

I can take Pie and me   to SoHo
to see this JMB guy

and Pie will ignore
the missed turns
the wrong notes
my lack of practice
at having
a friend.

* Jakoś to będzie (ya-KOSH-toh-BEN-jeh): Babcia taught Alina and
me this expression in Polish. It means things will work out in the
end, so you should be bold and act like things will work out.

GALLERY

I

Pie pauses at a boarded-up building
one block from the Spring Street
subway station

                    on plywood-covered windows
                    I read:

                    SAMO©
                    IS DEAD

words in funeral black
under a yellow crown.

"Who is Samo? How did he die?"

Pie calls me whack
which I think is the
opposite of cool.
But his lips turn up
in a smile
while he says it
so I wait for him
even though
Ms. Kirschbaum
is already waiting
for us.

II

The gallery charges money.
Pie has a card
that gets him in
for free   but I have nothing.
                                  No special card.
                                  No money.

Is that confusion on Pie's face?
Does he think because I'm white
I'm rich?

"Don't worry, JJ.
I have it covered,"
says Ms. Kirschbaum   and I search the desk
                                 her hands
                                 for whatever she's covering up.

"Just say thank you,"
Pie says.
And then I understand.

III

Inside looks like a store
but not one with toys
            or records
            or hardware.

The ceiling is as tall
as four people

standing
on each
others'
shoulders.

Paintings hang
on white walls.

Pie calls this a *gallery*
which is kinda like the museum
where I once went
on a school trip
but smaller
with no guide
to tell us
the paintings
are famous.

The museum was boring
but here
Pie's mouth hangs open
he sucks in his breath
with a *whoosh*
and I breathe in
fresh-sawed wood
           oil
           and pine.

Inside a rectangle
like a postage stamp
in the tall white-wall space

a bloody knife   SAMO's crown
points upward   floats above

the terrified goat
marked for sacrifice
in black and brown and
red
          giant bone
          beneath his hooves
  arrows pointing in
      directions   unknown

"SAMO is not dead,"   Pie whispers   but I can tell
                                                SAMO is angry.

          His skulls have sharp teeth
          Their open mouths scream
          Words scratched on canvas

"He has another name.
Jean-Michel Basquiat."   JMB

Jean-Michel Basquiat paints Pie's story
like Joe Strummer sings mine

              and this
              is my time
              to listen.

SOHO

no doubt
Brooklyn's the dopest borough
but there are four others in this city
millions of people call the Big Apple home
they don't know nothing 'bout how I live in Los Sures
and I don't know nothing 'bout how they live in their 'hood
I've never even been to Staten Island and only head
into Manhattan to visit my godbrother Andres
in June we meet up in Loisaida and head
downtown to show our Boricua pride
at the Puerto Rican Day Parade
at Christmas Uncle Lou once
took us to see Rockefeller's
fancy tree and the
wonderland windows
at Saks

I know
that to a lot of folks in this city
I'm nothing more than a flea
a pest they can't contain

a black speck of danger
they're determined
to crush

in SoHo
the only other people in
the gallery who look like me
are holding trays covered with
cheese cubes on toothpicks
or plastic cups filled
halfway with
red wine

I feel
the guard's eyes tracking me
like a laser as soon as we step
inside but JJ doesn't even
seem to notice
or care

at first
I think maybe that's

127

what it's like to be white
JJ's got his own personal force field
that keeps him safe and makes
him disappear whenever folks
are looking for someone
to blame

but then
I notice how he keeps
rubbing his hands on the front
of his jeans and I think maybe
his palms are just as
sweaty as mine

I wonder
if being in a place
like this ever makes
JMB feel like he's in
the wrong room

maybe that's
why his art is so bold

maybe each painting is
his way of giving the finger
to these old ladies in fur coats
and diamonds who would never
invite someone like him to
dinner but would pay big
bucks to hang his art
on their dining
room wall

some folks
in the gallery wear ripped
jeans and black leather jackets
their eyes hidden behind Ray-Bans
they sip wine and chomp cheese cubes
and laugh out loud like they got just as much
right to be here as the moneybags in mink
I look at all these people and then I see
Ms. K watching me and her smile
says there's room here for
someone like me

129

GREENPOINT

Wanna see my guitar?

not really
if I'm honest
but JJ's never asked me for nothing
he made me that mixtape that wasn't half bad
and it was kinda cool how he came down
to SoHo with us to check out the gallery
he wasn't freaked out by JMB's art and
he even asked some smart questions
which Ms. K says is more important
than knowing the right answer

so I say
will there be cookies?
and JJ *almost* laughs
he finally cracks a smile
before nodding so many times
I get a little dizzy
all right, man, let's go see
this amazing guitar
it better be special
the way you talk about it
all the time

we don't say much
on the train back to Brooklyn
I listen to his mixtape
he listens to mine
then we come out the subway and
I wonder if I've made a mistake

JJ's right—we're not that far from school
but Greenpoint feels like a whole other planet
an all-white world that feels foreign
and uncomfortable and maybe
not so safe
for me

If JJ senses the danger or notices
the way folks are staring glaring at me
he doesn't let on—he just heads up the street
and after three or four blocks we reach a flat-faced
row house with white aluminum siding and a bright red door
I head for the stairs—also painted red—but JJ waves me
over to the door under the stairs that leads to
the basement where his bob-chuh lives
that's Polish for grandma and as soon
as JJ turns his key in the lock
she's there in the doorway
her pink lips a small *o*
and her eyebrows
raised high above
her blue eyes

JJ introduces me as his friend
and that one word puts a smile on her face
soon she's bustling around the kitchen
it already smells like sugar and I see a plate
on the table that has a tea towel draped over it
could be kołaczki or some other Polish treat but
first we gotta do what we came here to do
JJ leads me to a corner of the living room
which is damp and dim with a ceiling
that hangs not too far from his head
I guess this is his bedroom or
at least where he sleeps
he takes the guitar

out of its case
strums a few
chords and
then

Give it here, JJ. Now.
Dad, this is Pie—I mean, Pierre.
I was just showing him . . .

His father's fist lands on the kitchen table
with so much force that the spoons jump
JJ jumps and I jump too
only his bob-chuh
doesn't flinch
but when JJ's dad speaks again
his voice is soft and low and that
makes him scarier somehow
Now, JJ, he says
holding out his hand
and JJ reluctantly peels off
his guitar and hands it over
Let's go, his dad says before
disappearing into a back room
and JJ follows him like a dog
with his head hanging down

It takes a full minute for me to
realize that JJ isn't coming back
I pick up my bag
sling it over my shoulder
and head for the door

I make it through the cast-iron gate that
separates their paved yard from the street
when I hear knuckles rapping on glass
I turn and there's his bob-chuh smiling

through the bars on the ground-floor window
she waves me back so I step into their yard
crowded with trash cans and wait until
she opens the front door to hand me a plastic bag
that holds something warm wrapped in foil
gift she says with a smile
that feels more like
an apology

I thank her and head for the train
desperately scanning the street for the glowing
green globes that mark the entrance to the subway
I want to book it back to my bloque but I'm afraid
of looking like I've done something wrong
just because I'm walking fast while Black

I have done nothing wrong
but no one around here looks like me
—I am invisible and yet I'm not 'cause
I am too dark & too different to disappear here
for the first time I wonder how JJ feels in the 'hood
if he learned how to be a ghost around me and my friends
or if he learned how to disappear
at home

133

SECOND SHADOW

I could be wrong
but I think JJ's been
following me

it's like being
stalked by a ghost
a white shadow that can
disappear in a crowd
or vanish even in
an empty room

it's weird but
there's something
about his silence that
doesn't seem strange
to me anymore

I guess I'm used
to him now so when I
come out of the museum
today feeling like an impostor
or some weird version of myself
that I don't recognize or even like
it's almost a relief to find JJ
sitting on the steps
waiting for me

I don't even
bother to ask
why he's
there

I just take his
friendship the
same way I take
the extra cookie
he always
brings to
lunch

we go over
to Prospect Park
between us we have
enough to buy two
hot dogs and a
can of Coke

we sit on the
wooden bench
that runs along the
curved wall of the
tunnel and talk
about art

how it makes us feel

how it can't be
locked in a dusty book or
cooped up in a museum

art belongs
in the street
I tell him

with the people
JJ adds

for a long
while we say
nothing just sit
there as the gray
sky beyond the
tunnel grows
dark

swallowed
by shadows
I tag the bench
with my Sharpie
JJ uses his house key
to carve his initials
into the wood to
prove that we
were here

OUTLAWS
by JJ Pankowski

When the laws don't make sense
You gotta climb the fence
[all] You gotta be an outlaw!

When the ones in charge are wrong
Can't wait for change for long
[all] You gotta be an outlaw!

Chorus:
You gotta be an outlaw
You gotta do what's right
You gotta be an outlaw
You gotta keep up the fight

Spray your paint up on the wall
Cause the mighty gonna fall
[all] You gotta be an outlaw!

The leaders of the past
Will show you how to act
[all] You gotta be an outlaw!

Chorus

THE OUTLAW SONG

I

Dad returns my guitar
          after I promise
          never to bring Pie
          home again.
"It's not me.
I worked with guys
          like him
          good union brothers
but your mom's gonna flip
and things aren't so great   between us
                        these days."

I nod
and believe it's over   and say okay

which doesn't mean
I won't find somewhere else
to meet Pie
with my guitar
and play my songs
with him.

II

I spend all week
          on my first song.

Hard to get right

                words
                chords
                rhythm

and how to ask someone
to not only be my friend
but start something with me too.

                Leader.

                            III

Friday
when the end of school bell rings
I tell Pie,
"I wrote a song for you."
Hand trembling
        I give him
        the paper.
"That 'leaders of the past' part
I was thinking of
                Patrice Lumumba
because he's not alive anymore.
You can shout out his name
when we sing that line."

"What are you talking about, JJ?"

                              I needed to start
                              at the beginning.

"I want to start a punk band
and you be in it
and if you know anyone else
they can be in it too."

Pie shakes his head.
"I don't own any instruments."

"I have a keyboard you
can borrow. My dad
doesn't care about it."

My face turns hot
because my dad did care.
I shouldn't have brought
Pie home. We should
have met in his neighborhood
or someplace in between
like Alina and I
still do.

Pie shakes his head even harder.
His chair screeches backward
and he joins the stampede
out the room

until Mr. Zullo calls,
"Velez!"

Pie turns his head
while his feet keep moving.

"I need your leader worksheet.
Monday. On my desk
or I'm deducting points."

I chase Pie through the hall
colors spinning around me
I know he finished his
worksheet. It's better
than mine.
catch him in the lobby.

                                        We already gave our report
                                        anyway.

Over his shoulder, he shouts,
"I don't have time
                    for a band,"
and I think I know why.

"Let me come with you
                    when you paint.
We can talk about it."

"Shhhh!" Pie yanks me toward him.
                                        I don't flinch.

"And the word is *BOMB*," he whispers.
He looks away, looks back.
"Meet me tonight at seven.
Lorimer Street double-L train.
Manhattan-bound side
in front of the token booth."

I don't walk home
                    but float
                    six inches above
                    the sidewalk.

I don't know where Pie wants to take me
but I'm ready to go
                    anywhere.

PAINT REMAINS

I

Zigzag block after block
south and west
underneath the Williamsburg Bridge
look out onto the East River
twinkling lights of Manhattan
we're in   Pie's neighborhood
            what
            he calls
            Los Sures

Pie carries his bag   with a lonely
                        paint can
                        to a wall
                        in an alley
                        moonlight shining
                        on broken sidewalk
                        cold tamping down
                        garbage smell.

He spray-paints the words
                        Somebody Got Murdered
from the Clash mixtape
I gave him
and below:
                        RIP Ricky

II

Paint remains
while music flies into the air
and disappears.

I pick up the can
              pop red plastic cap
heart thumping steady drumbeat
I shake the cold metal
to 8/8 time
              rattlerattlerattlerattle
squeeze the nozzle
                    pfft
Droplets the size of pinpricks
hurtle toward me.

I inhale
      sticky oil
            and cough.

"You're not doing it right," Pie says.

I know.
Because paint sticks to brick walls
blasts color into   gray skies
                          broken sidewalks
                          dingy subways
shouts *We are here*
and you can't shut us up!

TAG—I'M IT

maybe I was showing off   or maybe I just missed
     the way it feels to paint my name   across a wall
     to claim something   somewhere as my own for a while
sometimes JJ looks at me like   I'm different but in
     a good way   it might even be envy in his green eyes
     and maybe that's why I slipped into that alley
     unzipped my bag   shook the can   and wet the wall
with layers of red mist   made luscious loops in my
     signature style   maybe I was so caught up in creating and
     craving respect that I let my guard down broke the rules
forgot the food chain   let a predator catch me off guard
     sharks   never   sleep
     by the time I thought to run   it was too late
we were trapped in the alley   like rats   I had tossed the can
but the white cop still slammed me up against the wall   searched
     my pockets   my bag   called me a piece of s***
     said he was sick of animals like me   defacing public property
like anybody cares   what the walls of a stinking alley look like
     I wanted to say ain't it your job to   protect & serve
where were you when my boy Ricky   was shot down in the street
but I knew to   keep my mouth shut when   he found my ID
     said   *Brooklyn Museum*   *so you're a smart n***** huh*
I heard the jangle of metal handcuffs then the swirling lights
of a cop car filled   the alley with blue   red light
     I never heard him   call for backup but two more cops
     got out and joined the party   the pig was pressing my
     head into the wall
my cheek was red with wet paint   and the fumes made my eyes
     water but
     I could still see   that one was white and when the other one

looked at me I could tell   he was one of us   though the blue of his shirt

                and the light flashing off his badge   told me he was one of them too
he picked my ID up   off the ground read it   silently   then locked his eyes on mine

            I got this one, Kelly   *leave him with me*
        I got one cuff clamped on my wrist already   Kelly said *what?* like he was
ready to put his fist in that other cop's mouth   but he didn't back down

            take this one home   leave the other with me
        Kelly said *naw   I'm taking him in*   the other cop laughed
this runt ain't been in trouble before   and won't be again   right?
            that was my cue   *no sir*   I coughed out
        you're gonna take this punk's word for it?   gimme a break, Esposito

*trust me, Kelly   I know the family   he's more afraid of what
        his mother's gonna do to him when I knock on the door*

        he's pissing himself already   let him go
the hand pressing my face into the brick wall   gave one last shove before

            letting go   *that's your problem, Esposito   you're
too damn soft   we'll never clean up these streets   with your bleeding heart*

        not every thug deserves   a get-out-of-jail-free card
            *this one does   leave him with me   your shift's
almost over*

        you really want to spend an hour   filling out paperwork over this kid?

            I guess not 'cause Kelly took the cuff off my wrist   and sneered at me
before leading JJ   over to the car   uncuffed   of course
 c'mon, kid   let's get   you   back where you   belong
        Officer Esposito handed me back my ID asked where I live

and we began the long walk home I half listened to his long lecture
            enough to add   *yes sir*   now and then at least
and I really was grateful that he showed up and helped me out
            it could have ended differently   with me hog-tied and
in a coma at Bellevue
but all I could think about was how   through it all JJ   said nothing
        did nothing   just kept his head down   to keep himself safe
Andres was right no mixtape's gonna change   the system
                'cause when it comes to   playing tag with   cops
        they only ever   try to catch
                                someone like me

DIFFERENT JUSTICE

Flashing
        red   blue red   blue
                              lights
spin color into night sky.

Woop!
      One-bar siren . . .

Mouth dry
             my stomach teeters
                     on the edge
of sick.

Words stick to the back
of my teeth as
a third cop gets out
of a car still idling
slaps his holster
on the way toward me.

"Why are you here? This is
no place for a kid
        like
        you."

                        Think fast!

because they're shoving Pie
against the wall

                    slam his head
                    into wet paint

                                        and pain shoots
                                            down my
                                            neck
                                            spine
                                            legs.

        "We're friends from school, sir.
                            MS 126."
He was showing me
the river
the lights of
the Empire State Building
'cause I asked him to.

        "Get in the car.
        I'm taking you home."

                                        "M-my friend—?"
        "They're taking him in."

                                        He didn't do anything!

        Pie with the cops   Me with the cops
        arrested.   driven home.

                    Is this what Pie called
                    different justice?

MY OWN KIND

It's a silent ride
to Greenpoint
except for the police radio
                    crackling
                    a dozen
                    conversations
                    at once
that tell me nothing
about where they took Pie
                    or if they'll ever
                    let him go.

If the heat's on in the car
I don't feel it.

When I give my address
        voice wobbly
        teeth chattering
        whole body trembling
cop says, "You don't belong
where we caught you.
You need to make better friends.
Stick to your own kind."

I want to shake my head
except he'd see me in his
        rearview mirror.

                    My own kind
                    never wanted me
                    as a friend
                    never asked me

to come along
never made me feel
like I belonged
                    here
                    or
                    there.

Instead of those words
I squeak out a plea:

"Could you drop me off
at the end of my block?
My dad will kill me
if he saw me come home
                    in a police car."

"Sure thing."
                    The cop laughs.

                                        At my wimpy voice?
                                        My chattering teeth?
                                        My ghostlike face?

More questions:

Who exactly
is *my own kind*?
And who is the person
                    Alina says
I'm meant to be?

LOCKED DOWN

Officer Esposito says he won't come up so long as I promise
to stay out of trouble and I say I will but when I get upstairs

I hear the whir of a drill inside our apartment and open the
front door to find Tony putting a padlock on the outside of

Mami's bedroom door. It's for the best he tells Pilar before
spinning the last screw into the doorframe. This is the only

way to keep your mother safe. Pilar says nothing but when
she sees me—half my face painted red—she races across

the room and buries her face in my chest. *Where you been?*
Tony barks. *You call yourself the man of the house but where*

were you when your poor mother was walking the streets half
naked babbling like a . . . Tony's eyes land on Pilar and he bends

to put his drill back in the bag with the rest of his tools. *From*
now on this stays locked—¿entiendes? I put a bucket in there.

Empty it once a day but the rest of the time—whenever you
step out that door—this lock better be on. Got it, genius?

I don't understand but nod just so Tony will leave us alone.
He holds up the key to the padlock so I can see it and then

slams it on the kitchen counter like we're playing dominoes
but this ain't a game and part of me wants to run back down

stairs to get Officer Esposito—tell him my evil stepfather's
got my mother La Reina locked in a tower and I ain't no

prince or a knight in shining armor—I don't know how to
rescue my mother from her room or save her from herself

there's food in the fridge, Tony says—*make yourself useful and
fix your sister something to eat*. Like I don't do that every night.

Like I don't know how to take care of my family. Except I guess
he's right—I don't. Tony picks up his bag and says, *I gotta go to*

work. Plants a kiss on Pilar's head but just glares at me and then
he's gone. I do as I'm told but realize he didn't tell me to feed

Mami too. I fix her a plate, put the key in the padlock and take
her something to eat. Mami is curled up on her bed, shaking

even under the blanket. I can hear her whispering in Spanish
but she doesn't answer when I ask if she's hungry, so I just set

the plate on top of her dresser and pull the door closed behind
me. I leave the padlock dangling open—no reason to lock my

mother in her room when I'm here to keep an eye on her. Tony
said to lock it whenever I left the house but this is our home not

a prison and I am her son not her jailer. What's more important?
Being safe or being free? Tomorrow is Saturday so I don't have to

worry about school and thanks to Tony there's food in the house.
So all I gotta do this weekend is keep Pilar happy and keep Mami

inside the apartment. After we do the dishes I tell Pilar to go get
the cards and we play Go Fish till it's time for bed. I sleep on the

sofa in the living room so I can see the front door. I wasn't here
when Mami needed me most. I won't ever let that happen again.

I LIE

everyone thinks Mami is such a great cook
     and she was
          everything I know about food I learned from her
   Mami used to throw down in the kitchen
             but those days are long gone
if I give you a plate of sancocho
     and your mouth starts to water (trust me—it will)
          it's not Mami you should thank
   it's me
               these days it's me
doing all the shopping
   and all the cooking
   and all the cleaning
        not trying to complain
          after all I'm the man of the house and Pilar
she tries to help out
   she's too quiet my sister
        she should laugh more
   but instead Pilar creeps up beside me and asks
          will I be like Mami when I grow up?
I lie every time
to wipe the fear from my little sister's blue eyes
                    I lie

COPS & ROBBERS
by JJ Pankowski

You heard of cops and robbers
You played it as a kid
But did you really think about
Just what that robber did?

Could he have swiped a loaf of bread
To feed his family?
Or bombed a rainbow on the wall
For all the world to see?

Chorus:
Who's the cop?
Who's the robber?
Who's the good guy?
Who's the bad?
Is there different justice
From the justice that we have?

And why does it have to happen
The color of your skin
Would make the biggest difference
The trouble that you're in?

Cop told me stick to my own kind
To keep outta trouble
But I do what I wanna do
Though the trouble's double
(segue into "Should I Stay or Should I Go")

PLAGIARISM

Over the weekend
I put the words
to a reggae beat
like "Police & Thieves"
but not exactly

because Mr. Zullo called it
plagiarism

                     when he told me
                     to put Lech Wałęsa's biography
                     in my own words

                     and not call him Lech
                     because he's not
                            my friend.

GHOSTING THE GHOST

I'm not saying it's his fault. We don't
get to choose the skin we're in. Kids
who look like JJ are just born with a

get-out-of-jail-free card. Maybe I'm to
blame. After all—I'm the one who let
him into my life. It was me who chose

to share my world. I let this strange kid
see a side of me I usually keep to myself.
I trusted him even though my own people

told me to be careful. They are the ones
who love me. They are the ones who've
always got my back. I need them and they

need me to make the right choices 'cause
when I screw up it's not just me who pays
the price. My family needed me that night

and I wasn't there. I was too busy giving JJ
a tour of the 'hood. I took that white boy
for a walk on the wild side but he wound

up safe at home 'cause the NYPD's set up
to protect and serve people like him. JJ
thinks he's a rebel with a cause but he didn't

lift a finger to help me when I was slammed
up against that wall. He just walked away. Got
in that car like he was cool with having a cop

for a chauffeur. Like he actually believed he
needed to be saved from someone like me.
I could have been arrested. Put in the system.

Taken away from my family forever. And for
what? I risked it all for some kid who thinks he
understands how the world works just 'cause

he listens to songs sung by a bunch of white
dudes who lifted their best beats from guys
who look like me. They got played too, so

I guess I'm not the only sucker out here.
Maybe that's the real reason I'm so mad.
Maybe I've been avoiding JJ 'cause every

time I see the regret in his eyes I remember
how small and scared and alone I felt that
night. What good is a too-late apology from

a so-called friend who makes me feel that way?

CLASH

when my godbrother
calls to tell me he got
the tickets I asked him for
I don't tell him he was
right about white boys

        Andres used to work at the movie theater
        and sometimes he let me and Pilar in for free
        I wanted to see *Poltergeist* but I knew my little
        sister couldn't handle all that supernatural stuff
        so instead we saw *E.T.* three times in one day
        I guess Andres let in too many of his friends
        'cause he got fired from the cinema and now
        he works security at some club on
        the Lower East Side

when JJ kept talking about the Clash
I asked my godbrother what he thought of the band
Andres said he wasn't really into the punk-rock scene but
they seemed pretty cool for a bunch of white boys from England
even if they did steal their beats from Jamaican musicians
who wouldn't ever get the same chance to tour the world

        I looked at the floor when Andres asked
        you hanging with white boys now?
        then he shrugged and said
        some of them is cool
        but watch yourself, bro
        they may dig our beats
        and try to bite our style
        but at the end of the day

> *they can put on a suit and tie*
> *and bounce past the cops*
> *just like Clark Kent*
> *dig me?*

now I got JJ stalking me
at school but I don't wanna
hear what he's got to say

true friends
don't leave you
hanging

true friends
always have
your back

NOT FAIR

I

Mr. Zullo lays our graded projects
                    facedown
                    on our desks

my handwritten pages
stapled to
the sheet with his comments
on the oral reports
we gave   ten days ago
                    before the tagging
                    and the police
                    when we were still speaking
                    and Pie and I
                    interviewed each other
                    about our leaders.

                    His idea.

My own voice sounded strange
                    at first
but I can't shut up
when I talk about
what I like best

                                        even if Lech Wałęsa
                                        is not
                                        my friend.

I think I did okay   at least a B

            but

did Mr. Zullo mark down
every misspelled word
                    every stutter

                                        the fact that he had to
                                        cut me off
                                        at the end?

Mouth too dry to swallow
I hold my breath
until purple spots
break-dance across
the lined back page.

                                        Please be a B!
                                        I worked so hard . . .

Fingers numb
I flip the pages . . .

                                        A+

                    A+ ???

My first   A+   ever!

"Not fair!"

My head jerks
                    to the right.

Pie waves his report
                    three pages
                    thicker
                    than mine.

Mr. Zullo's lips quiver
in the moment
before he speaks:

"Do you have a problem, Velez?"

The class goes silent
waiting . . .

I cover my A+
with my hand.

                                        Don't want Pie
                                        to see it.

                                        Don't want Mr. Zullo
                                        to take it away

because Pie's report
                    on Patrice Lumumba
was way better
than mine.

He had more sources
                    like real books
                    not just the encyclopedia
                    and three newspaper articles
                    Mr. Zullo
                            asked for.

His oral report
used bigger words.

I learned things
I'd never heard
            before
                    like how our government
                    killed Patrice Lumumba
                    and broke up his movement
                    that freed the people
                    of Congo

the same way
the Soviets invaded Poland
and broke up Solidarity
and President Reagan
broke up my dad's union.

Pie told me to dig deeper
but he
dug
deepest
of all.

II

"Velez, your grade won't change
no matter how hard
you stomp your foot,"

Mr. Zullo says

but that's unfair
because Pie
didn't actually
stomp
his
foot.

He only said that Mr. Zullo
had made
a mistake.

Do I tell Mr. Zullo
I never saw Pie
stomp his foot
and he worked hard
on his project?

Or do I take my A+

                    straight home
                    to Babcia and Mom
                    and Dad and Uncle Russell?

Not take the chance
that Mr. Zullo made a mistake
that the C I spied
                    at the top
                    of Pie's paper

belonged to me
and my A+
belonged to him.

III

Mr. Zullo is scary
and I don't deserve the A+
any more than I deserved
to go home last week

                    while Pie
                    was arrested.

This is my chance
to set it right.

I wait for the bell to ring
slide my report in my backpack
to make it harder
for Mr. Zullo
to change
the grade.

He's packed his things
stands at the door
about to turn out the lights
when I catch him.

"Mr. Zullo," I say
out
loud.

"What?"

"Pie's right.
The grade you gave him.
Not fair."

His eyes cut into me.
His words cut deeper.
"You got your A plus.
What more do you want?"

"B-but . . ."

My words echo   in the dark empty classroom
like I stood up for Pie   to no one.

A Sidebar from My Report

Anna Walentynowicz

The strike began on August 14, 1980, after one of Lech Wałęsa's best friends was fired from the Lenin Shipyard in Gdańsk. The friend's name is Anna Walentynowicz (VAL-en-tih-NO-veech). She drove a crane at the shipyard and helped Lech Wałęsa start Solidarity. After the government broke the strike and banned Solidarity, they arrested her along with him and put them both in jail. But they didn't get to go to jail together because they always put boys on one side of the jail and girls on the other.

HEY, COLONIZER

a thousand years
before Columbus
reached our shores
looking for gold
we called our
island home
Borinquén

"land of the great lords"

when the Taíno
refused to be slaves
they were tortured and killed
by the Spaniards who went
to Africa next looking for
replacements

a few hundred years later
the king of Belgium wanted
a slice of Africa so he stole it and
took all the rubber he could get by
making the Congolese work for
him for next to nothing

ten million
lives snuffed out
to make one greedy
man filthy rich

here in the US of A
Mr. Zullo talks about

manifest destiny but he
don't have much to say
about the Trail of Tears or how
Yanqui soldiers invaded Puerto Rico back
in 1898 and picked up right where Spain left off
Zullo tells us to pick a leader
we admire but just 'cause
Jackson's on every
twenty-dollar bill
don't make him
a hero to me

Mr. Ashrawi says our destiny is to resist
Tía Rosa says the last shall be first
Uncle Lou says Whitey better
watch out 'cause sometimes
the empire strikes back

I say
hey, colonizer
why don't YOU go back
where you came from
but before you leave
give us back all
the things you
stole

our land
our language
our way of life
our gods
our hands
our dignity

FOR THE RECORD

all I did was shove my textbook off the edge of my desk/it weighs a ton so it hit the floor with a bang that made Zullo jump like the punk he is/was I mad? HELL YEAH/but it's not like I jumped him or nothing/ next thing I know he's foaming at the mouth and hollering at me to take my bad attitude someplace else/but I don't need a lecture from the principal right now so I grabbed my bag and stormed outta school/ went by the garden looking for Tito but the chain was on the gate so I just walked off my anger before heading home/wish I *had* hurled that brick of a book at Zullo's big head/I didn't but the principal ain't gonna believe me no matter what I say/he'll take his side and insist I must have earned the big red C Zullo scrawled at the top of my report/I had those kids on the edge of their seats talking 'bout roots and revolution/Zullo musta figured he'd put me back in my place with that bogus grade but no letter can tell me what my mind is worth/I won't beg or try to plead my case/ain't no justice here in Los Sures/just us

> *don't push me*
> *'cause I'm close to the edge*
> *I'm trying not to lose my head . . .*

THE MAN

the only thing worse than
getting a grade I don't deserve
on the best paper I've ever written
is coming home to find that Mami is GONE
and it's all my fault 'cause I didn't lock
her up like Tony told me to

she'd been feeling better the past
couple weeks—more like her old self

> cooking
> cleaning
> laughing with Pilar
> as they tried to
> moonwalk across
> the kitchen floor

then someone flicked the switch in her brain
and Mami went out into the world without a map
or a guide and no one to steer her back to safety
to make matters worse Tony decides to stop by
on his way to work and it's only the fact that
I'm holding Pilar in my arms that stops her
father from putting his hands on me
he's that mad

> *How long she been gone?*
> *I don't know*
> *what you mean YOU DON'T KNOW*

I want to say I'm just a kid, Tony,
I been at school all day but instead
I stare at the floor and press my lips together
so he won't see that I'm shaking inside

> *you think those A's make you special*
> *but school's just a waste of time*
> *pendejo*
> *all you had to do was*
> *turn the key in the lock*
> *but you think you're so smart*
> *smarter than me, right?*
> *well, I ain't hunting her down again*
> *she's your mother so*
> *get out there and find her*
> *GO! ¡VAMOS!*

I try to unwrap Pilar's arms
but she won't let go so Tony tries
yanking her by the shoulders but that only
makes things worse 'cause Pilar starts to cry and I start
to get mad *don't touch my sister I'll do whatever the*
hell I want—she's my daughter that don't give you the
right to grab her like that let go of her
I said LET GO OF HER

I don't know just what happens next
if I push Tony or if he pulls Pilar
if it's Tony's elbow or fist that finds my face
but when Pilar sees the blood she screams

Mr. Ashrawi must hear the commotion 'cause when
I finally reach the hallway sopping up the blood with
my sleeve my sister's screams are still echoing in my head

the door to his apartment is open and he stops me before
I fly down the stairs hands me a towel tells me to tip my
head back while he calls Uncle Lou who shows up in no
time I follow him and Marta back into our apartment and
she holds Pilar while I change my shirt and get ready to hit
the streets to search for Mami but then I hear a crash and when
I come back out to the living room Tony's on the floor and
Uncle Lou's shaking his hand out and cursing in Spanish
you ever lay a hand on Pierre again and you're dead—hear me?

DEAD

Uncle Lou goes over to Mami's room takes the open padlock off its hook
and hurls it at Tony's head like he's Luis "Mambo" DeLeón

NOW GET THE F*** OUT

Tony picks himself up off the floor rubbing his head and cursing
under his breath and when he stops in front of Marta to collect Pilar
she just shakes her head how could he think Pilar would leave with him
after everything he's done? Once he's gone Uncle Lou takes a deep breath
and looks at me, his eyes shining with sadness
Why didn't you tell me, papi?
I don't know if he means the lock or Mami getting lost in the street
I have been holding in so many secrets that my face starts to hurt
then the room starts swimming and I feel my legs start to sway
when I open my mouth to answer my tío
all that comes out is a sob

but before I can fall
Uncle Lou wraps
me in his arms
he holds me up
tucks my head

under his chin
and lets me cry
I hear him whisper
I got you, papi
just hold on to me
you don't gotta
be the man
no more

BE A FRIEND

Pie still won't speak to me.

It's been two weeks   of the silent   treatment
of me fading
into the blackboard
that covers the left-side wall
of the classroom   my usual seat
again alone
again invisible

        ghost
      with no head
        space
      for lessons
        only
      questions

Why did Mr. Zullo cheat Pie?
Why didn't I do enough for my friend?
What would Lech Wałęsa think
        of me?

        Because he climbed a fence
        to lead that strike
        after they fired
          his friend.

I can't lead a strike
        but
I can say I'm sorry
even if it won't

        change
        anything.

The bell rings.
I chase Pie out of class   school   through Williamsburg streets

past now-familiar shops
under the expressway
into the subway station
flash student pass
push through the gate
downstairs to the LL
                    platform.

                                        Me always ten feet behind him.

"Quit following me!
Go home, pendejo!"

                                        "I'm sorry about your grade.
                                        You should have gotten an A."
"It doesn't matter!"

                                        "Yes, it does! You won't make
                                        high honor roll this time."

"It. Doesn't. Matter.
Get it?"

I don't
but after the train takes him away
I think
I do.

175

I AM NOT JOE STRUMMER

I

Joe Strummer would write a song.

Not as good as starting a strike
to protect a friend.

I wrote two songs already
and they changed
nothing.

Pie once said he liked my music.
Does that count as   something?

On my way home
I piece words together
like a 3D puzzle.

II

I unlock the door
drop my backpack
reach for my guitar
but my fingers find only air
my eyes
        the water-stained wall.

"Dad!"

First potbelly
then the rest of him
fills the kitchen archway
over his shoulder
shaggy-haired Uncle Russell
beer fumes around them
like Pigpen's dust.

"My guitar.
Where is it?"

"It's not *your* guitar."

A loan . . .
I hadn't believed him.
Hope pours out with each
heart
beat.

"What did you do
with it?"

"We needed it. That's all
you need to know."

"Uncle Russell?"

He nods
behind my dad.
Not going to stand up for me
any more than
          I stood up for Pie.

I am not Joe Strummer.

No guitar
just a half-dozen picks
on the threadbare carpet
and minor chords
strumming adagio
in my head.

BLACK FRIDAY

The noise
of a thousand Black Friday shoppers
screams, *Run!*

The blinking
of a hundred Christmas lights
a warning sign: *Hide!*

I force my legs
      to stand
      rooted
      on the
hard   marble
floor   of this
              mall
halfway between
Alina   and   me.

In front of me
the guitar store.

Behind me
my sister

so much of
what I had   once upon
                a time.

Alina talks about school
      the basketball team
      Claire.

"I figured you'd understand,"
she says. "You have a curious
mind. Rules don't hold you down
like they do for others."

She ruffles my hair
breathes hot peppermint into my face.
I grind my sneaker's toe
into the hard mall floor.
That shoe's gonna need duct tape
                        soon
                        too.

"Something's bothering
you, JJ," she says. "You
don't hide things so good either."

                        Busted.

I point to the guitar store window.

                        "Last Tuesday
                        when I got home from school
                        my guitar was gone.
                        Dad and Uncle Russell said
                        they needed it."

"They probably sold it
because they're broke."

                        Broken.

I stare at a black-and-white
Gibson Les Paul.

                        "Uncle Russell said it was his
                        first guitar."

"Sounds like they're desperate."

I make out the price tag.
So many numbers . . .

                        "But I was in the middle
                        of writing a song. For a
                        friend,"

who I don't think
is a friend
anymore.

"I wish I could buy
you a new one.
But I'm a kid too
and there's only so much
a kid can do."

Her hand on my shoulder
makes me jump.
For a moment I look into her eyes.
They glisten red and green
as if she's crying
and her tears reflect
store windows
and Christmas lights.

"Keep the faith, little brother.
I promise one day
I will."

How do you keep the faith
when all you can do
is get on the train
empty-handed
and walk the rest of the way home
one foot
after the other?

One foot after the other . . .
A rhythm
in search of a melody

away from the crowd
the music
inside of me.

FINGERS GROWN SOFT

Casio keyboard's
still in the box
from the night
we fled Lynbrook.

I fish fresh batteries
from the kitchen drawer
not looking at anyone
not answering their questions
    like:
      "Where did you go
      today?"

          "He's become so moody,"
          says Mom at the table
          and Dad
          guitar stealer
          stays silent.
          No one translates
          for Babcia
          making us klopsiki
          for dinner.

I inhale the warm rich aroma
of sizzling meatballs
list the good things
in my life:
Babcia
her cooking
Pie   my first friend
even if he

called me a name
in Spanish
and told me to
go away.

I can still write
my song for him
hope that he'll
forgive me
because Christmas is coming
and New Year's
time for fresh starts.

Sitting cross-legged on my cot
I turn my back to the kitchen
plug in my headphones
flip the switch.

The hum is a blank page
                    beckoning my hands to press keys
                    just wide enough
                    for fingers grown since summer.

No guitar like Joe Strummer
only me JJ

who won't be the next Chopin
but softening fingertips
touch compact keys
remember metronome beat
                    scales
                    melodies

feel the power in my hands
                    my heart
                    my song
                    my story.

TRIGGER

I always thought a trigger was the deadliest part of a gun
the part you can't take back, the part that sends a bullet

out of the barrel and into a body or my boy Ricky's back but
Mr. Ashrawi's daughter Seren is a social worker and she says

Mami gets sicker when something upsets her or reminds her
of a time when she didn't feel safe or wasn't in control. Turns

out getting a call from a cousin back home telling her my abuelo
had a stroke is the trigger that sent Mami out of the apartment

and into the street thinking she had to reach her sick father
before anything else bad happened to him. Seren sits us down

and explains that Bellevue, the hospital where she works, won't
admit Mami unless it's an emergency so that's why she called for

the ambulance even though Mami was calm by the time the cops
brought her home after spotting her walking up the ramp of the BQE.

It's a good thing our address was on the suitcase Mami took with her
though it was only half packed. Once Marta got her cleaned up, Mami

looked just like she used to before the sickness in her head filled
the world with invisible triggers that anyone could pull, even the

people who love her. The ambulance pulled up in front of our building
its lights swirling but no siren to signal to the neighbors that we were

in crisis. A few people stopped to watch the paramedics lead Mami out of our building. She climbed into the back of the ambulance and

had just enough time to wave and smile weakly at me and Pilar as we stood on the sidewalk watching our family fall apart. Now Pilar

sits next to me on the couch, her blue eyes dry, her fingers wrapped tight around mine. The adults are talking about us but not to us and

we both know what that means. They're making plans, shaping our future like we're two lumps of clay that need grown-ups to mold us

into happy children. I know it's only a matter of time before Tony shows up to claim Pilar but I can tell by the tilt of my sister's chin

that Pilar isn't planning on going anywhere without me. Tony's a jerk but he loves Pilar and if she went to live with him, she'd have

everything she needs. I love her, too, but I have to do what's best for what's left of my family so when I hear Uncle Lou arguing with

Tía Rosa over who should be the one to go home and take care of Abuelo, I clear my throat and say, "I'll go with you. Take me, too."

ECHO

When we were friends
before I didn't stand up to the cops
or change Mr. Zullo's mind
before I lost my guitar

Pie showed me
the cutaway fence
the kid-size gap
between padlocked
McCarren Park pool house doors.

I tagged the basement walls,
he said. *It's dark and echoey*
but I wasn't scared.

If I'm not scared
if I walk the places that Pie walked
see his hieroglyphics like SAMO's

I can write my song for him
and he will want to be my friend
                                    again.

I tell Dad I have homework at the library
pack keyboard
        flashlight
        notebook
slip through gap
            down
                broken
                    stairs

                                    to
                              deserted
                                          dark
                                          basement
                                                      stinking
                                                                  of
                                                      mildew
                                                                        and
                                                                        chlorine

shine light on crumbling concrete walls
listen for voices:
                        Pie
                              or other kids
                                          or ghosts

Am I the only ghost down here?

Do I imagine Pie's spray can?
                        rattlerattlerattle
                        HISS!
                                          7/8 time

Crouched against a column
keyboard balanced across my knees
I play through cheap built-in speakers
notes that bounce off metal and concrete.
No   voices
          guitar
          drums
          cowbells
          or two-by-fours on garbage cans

but some songs need no words
and echo is its own
          backbeat.

OUT OF TIME

there's no time for long goodbyes
and that's fine by me/a relief even
better to make a clean break so
I can have a fresh start back home
I was born here in Brooklyn but
these days I feel like the bloque
isn't big enough for who I want
to be

Manny and Oz came by last night
gave me a bunch of comic books
to read on the plane and a brown
paper bag full of Now and Laters
Andres stopped by too to drop off
the tickets I don't need anymore
thought about tossing them in the
trash but put them in an envelope
instead and tucked it inside my bag

our flight leaves at noon so I get up
early and go to school to clear out
my locker and stop by the art room
one last time to tell Ms. K how much
I appreciate everything she's done for
me/I'm gonna miss the last few weeks
of art camp and I haven't finished my
final project but Uncle Lou says there
are museums and plenty of artists on
the island/I'm sure I can learn just as
much from them/maybe even more

the door is open but I knock anyway
Ms. K looks up and smiles at me like
she always does/I try to smile back
but something in my face must tell
her I'm not here to stay/Ms. K points
to the chair next to her desk/I take a
seat and she listens as I tell her about
Mami going to Bellevue and Abuelo
having a stroke/she says, *Oh, Pierre*

it doesn't feel like pity when Ms. K
reaches over and gives my arm a
squeeze/then she pulls herself up
grabs her cane and leads me over
to the supply closet/Ms. K tells me
to open my bag and I don't say a
word as she drops a few brushes/
several drawing pencils/glue/a jar
of gold glitter and several tubes of
paint inside

    make something phenomenal she
    says/I manage to choke out a thank-
    you before the tears start to fall/then
    I see the envelope at the bottom of
    my bag so I pull it out and hand it to
    her/Ms. K looks at the two letters I
    scrawled on it and says, *he's really
    going to miss you*

        I just shrug and zip up my bag but Ms. K
        isn't done with me yet/she pushes her
        glasses up the narrow bridge of her nose
        and says *sometimes people come into our
        lives for a reason/but only for a season*

I nod to show that I heard her words then
I check the clock on the wall and give Ms.
K a quick hug before slipping out of the
school just as the bell rings

PIE'S MESSENGER

I

Pie doesn't show up at school
on Monday
and when he doesn't show up
on Tuesday

I think he's sick
but his two friends
the ones he calls Manny and Oz
are hanging around
his locker
staring at the floor
like I always do.

I take a step backward
flatten myself against
pale cinder-block wall
and listen to their words:

Bellevue
Hospital
mother

II

I never say much to Ms. Kirschbaum
even though
I eat in her art room
every Tuesday and Thursday.
She mainly talks with the art kids

and that's my time
to listen to music.

But I'm worried enough to ask her
and even more worried
when she brings me
to her office.

She leans her door shut.
"I'm so sorry, JJ,"
she says. "Pierre had to go away.
He won't be coming back
for a long time."

A punch to the gut.
Fingers squeezing my throat.
"I heard these other kids
say something.
About his mother
and Bellevue Hospital
wherever that is.
Why didn't he tell me?
I thought we were friends.
A friend would tell a friend
if he was going away forever
                    wouldn't he?"

                                        He told Manny and Oz.
                                        I guess they were his real friends.
                                        Not me.

"Yes. Pierre had a family situation.
He'll have to tell you
                    about it
                    himself.
It's not my business."

A family situation?
I have a family situation.
I didn't tell anyone.
Not even Pie.

"He wanted you to have this."
She hands me an envelope
with the letters *JJ*
in Pie's handwriting.

I drop it into my backpack
rub my face with my sleeve
which leaves my cheeks wet and sticky
and hot with shame
for crying in school.

Ms. Kirschbaum stands with her cane.
She steps toward me
like she wants to put her arm
around my shoulders.

                              Do I let her?

She tells me
art shines light in the darkness
art gives voice
        to what we can't say in words
art brings us together
        no matter who we are.

"Pierre told me you compose music.
He said you wanted to start a band."

She motions me to follow.
She is young yet moves slowly like Babcia.
At the end of the hallway
she unlocks a door

into a room shimmering
with instruments

> guitars
> piano
> double-deck synthesizer
> with full-size keyboard
> for my growing hands
> for all the songs
> I want to write.

"Next semester
you can add music
to your schedule
and every Tuesday and Friday
some kids in a punk-rock band
practice after school."

I lift an electric guitar
feel its weight in my hands.

"You already know Damaly and Maya.
They eat lunch in the art room with you."

> Yes, I've seen them.
> Damaly: light-skinned
> hair shorter than mine
> Maya: medium brown skin
> ponytail, pink backpack
>
> I've never talked to them.

"Do they really want someone new?"

> Will they like me?
> Can I fit in?

Be part of something
other people started?
Make new friends
and not lose them
this time?

"They said they did.
But I'm going
to let you talk to them
because it should come from you
and not me."

Yes   No
No   Yes

I can
talk
to new
people.
I can
try out.

I can
try.

PALIMPSEST

I knew what it meant before I started going to the museum but
those white kids almost got whiplash turning their heads so fast/
eyes popping from hearing a word like that coming outta the mouth
of a boy like me/sitting smug at the back of the room/I schooled
them that day/giving props to Ms. K since she's the one who broke it
down for me/my tongue tumbled over that weird word in one of her
art magazines/it's like how JMB scribbles over surfaces that already
have stuff written on them so you see his words along with the ones
underneath/a story on top of another story/I been knowing for a
while that life is all about layers/peel them back and you'll see the
people that came before us/places too/before Tito grew his garden
there was an empty lot filled with trash and before that there was a
building on that corner/home to dozens of families from places like
Palestine and Puerto Rico/land free and then Columbused and then
colonized/waiting to be free once more/Taíno/Spanish/African/Boricua/
Nuyorican/blood blended/languages lost and learned/though some
words linger on tongues taught to pray to new gods along with the
old/and up on the roof the space on the wall I saved for Ricky has been
tagged so many times I can't even see my boy's name anymore/I ain't
mad/Ricky's got company now/other boys resting in peace on the wall/
our dead like seeds we bury by moonlight beneath layers of paint/
graffiti spreads like spores/spawning new styles to tell stories that cross
bridges to bloom in other boroughs and beyond/now I am high above
the clouds/buckled in between Pilar and Tía Rosa/she says we'll be
back before the new year begins/tells us Mami will be better by then/I
hope she's right but keep my doubts to myself/for now I guess we
gotta trust the doctors to find out what's wrong/give them a chance
to help my mother/at least keep her safe/somebody has to show Mami
how to find the self she lost to the lying voices in her head/I need to
clear mine too/not like shaking an Etch A Sketch/don't need my screen

wiped clean/never was nobody's blank slate/I am a palimpsest/my
short story is written on top of a longer tale that began before my
family came to Brooklyn/I want to see the parts Mami and her siblings
tried to overwrite by starting a new chapter in Nueva York/I'm going
back to Borinquen/not to conquer but to care for my abuelo/and learn
about my people/in their candy-colored houses/in the
cobbled streets of Old San Juan/in the green fields full of coffee and
cane/I am digging for my roots/someday I'll fly across the sea to Africa/
dig there too till I've found my father/for now Uncle Lou says Africa
lives in Loíza/never been there before/so much to explore/I close my
eyes and see the sea/weaving between waves is a mermaid with skin
like mine/but she ain't about to swap her voice just to be with some
dude/check the machete in her hand/on the island we got
our own stories/and can write our own endings/don't care it we gotta
tear the pages outta their textbooks/scratch out the lies and set the
record straight/we are like trees that survive the lash of the hurricane
by holding on to the land/branches may break off/leaves may fall/but
life persists/we resist/insist on getting back up no matter what/the way
I see it/this trip is my declaration of independence/give me liberty or
watch me take what's mine/don't got no more time for Zullo and his
kind/I wanna look in the mirror and like love what I see/this Black boy/
genius/artist/is breaking outta his box

STOOD UP

I

At home
in the bathroom   door locked
                       hands trembling
I peel open the envelope.

Did Pie send me his address?
                If so
                I would write him
                tell him all the things
                I should have said
                tell him I'm sorry
                about his mom
                tell him I wish I'd known
                even if I couldn't have done anything
                at least I could have brought them
                kołaczki.

I lift out two pieces of paper.
No address.
No note to explain.
Only tickets.

What?

Tickets!

THE CLASH
IN CONCERT

this Friday!

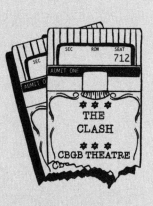

like Pie planned to invite me
                  but couldn't
like he wanted to be my friend
                  but couldn't

                                  now I want to thank him
                                  but can't.

II

I can't sneak out like Alina did last year
when she told Mom she was spending the night at Claire's house
and Claire told her mom she was spending the night with us
and they took the train from Lynbrook to Manhattan
to see a concert at that same punk-rock club

so I ask Uncle Russell in private
pretend I'm not angry he sold my guitar
show him the tickets.

"My friend Pie from school gave me these.
He couldn't go
so maybe you can."

He jerks his head backward.
calls out, "Oi, Marcin!
Look what the kid showed up with!"

So much for *in private* . . .
Dad clomps into the living room.

"He said a mate gave these to him.
Didn't know Joey had a mate."

"It's that colored kid."
Dad glares at me. I feel the heat

even though I avoid his eyes.
"Didn't I tell you
not to have anything
to do with him
again?"

"You told me not to bring him here.
And there's no *again*
because he's gone to Puerto Rico."

"Don't get smart with me!"
Dad pulls back his hand
like he's gonna slap me
and for a second I think
Uncle Russell will grab his arm
and protect me
                    but no

                              I can't count on Uncle Russell
                              any more than Pie could count
                              on me.
                              I can only count on myself now.

"Why aren't you happy
I had a friend for once?
A friend who got way better grades
than I do?"

I suck in my breath.

"That project I got an A plus on?
He helped me with it
even after *you* kicked him out."

I step away
though Dad's hand
doesn't move toward me.

"And you know what else I saw?
Babcia went out there
                in the cold
and gave him the kołaczki she made
like she thought you were rude
and wanted to say sorry
for all of us."

Dad's hand drops to his side.

"Gobsmacked," Uncle Russell says
and I raise my clenched fist
because I am too.

"I'll go with him, Marcin.
Keep an eye on the boy-o.
Make sure he's not smashed like a bug
in the pogo dancing."

"Yeah, you do that, Russ."

I've never stood up to Dad before
on my feet
        tall
him hunched over
slinking away
like that light-skinned bully Pie dropped
with one hammer drumbeat
                        but
mine was words
I never said before
words I should have said before
but still
the right words
for now.

THE MAGNIFICENT SEVEN

Except for Damaly
and Maya
I've never seen these kids.
The other four are big
eighth graders.

Will they accept me?
                Like me?
                        Think I'm any good?

                                    I've never made a team
                                    or anything else
                                    I've tried out for.

And how can I play for a punk band
when Uncle Russell had to sit with me
far away   in the balcony
because I couldn't stand the noise
                or the crowds
                by the stage?

What to say to these kids?

"Hi. I'm JJ."

                                    [weak wave]

I won't remember their names

                                    unless I attach them
                                    to instruments.

Aníbal   lead guitar
Damaly   vocals
Ernie   rhythm guitar

Maya	bass
Victor	keyboards
Zoraida	drums

They don't need another guitar
but Victor wants to play trumpet

> and if I agree
> to play what they tell me
> the band they call
> The Magnificent Seven
> will have its seven

and I'll be part of a band
named after a Clash song
the first song on side two
of the first mixtape
I gave Pie.

(They sang it at the concert
last weekend
and I wonder if Joe Strummer
was ever this scared
when he went onstage.)

I rock on the bench
hunch over the keyboard
shake out my hands
wipe sweaty palms on my jeans
flip the switch
touch fingertips to keys
pause at the first note
that fills the room
                    breathe.

Chopin's Polonaise no. 6
the dreaded song
they used to make me play
over and over

        until I got it right
flows to my fingers
as if in my Polish blood
        then

            segues

                into the insistent forward beat
                of "London Calling"

First guitars
then bass
and drums
join in
Damaly grabs the microphone
and we jam until the sun sets
on one of the shortest days of the year
smash completely different
             songs together   like chemistry
                     like magic
                     to make something new.

          Not:
          brown or white
          Puerto Rican or Polish
          girls or boys
          normal or weird
          eighth or seventh
               graders

But:
GuitarsBassDrumsKeyboardsTrumpetVoice

          because music
          brings us together
          no matter who
          we are.

MIXTAPE #2/AUDITION TAPE
FOR DAMALY AND MAYA

Side One	Side Two
"Know Your Rights"—The Clash	"Golden Brown"—The Stranglers
"I Fought the Law"—The Clash	"Golden Brown" instrumental
"English Civil War"—The Clash	(JJ playing)
"Dancing Barefoot"—Patti Smith	"McCarren Park Underground"
"Gloria"—Patti Smith	—JJ Pankowski instrumental
"Ask the Angels"—Patti Smith	"The Outlaw Song"—JJ Pankowski
"Ain't It Strange"—Patti Smith	"Cops & Robbers"—JJ Pankowski

THE ONES WHO STAY

I used to believe
        paint remains
while music flies into the air
        and disappears.

Now I know.

A mural can be painted over
and music is more than sound waves
        etching on plastic platters
        particles on acetate.

It's people who come together
        instruments
        the tools
        we carry
        with us.

The ones who leave
go out looking
for what they don't have

                        but

the ones who stay
are the ones who change
the places where
we are.

Our band rehearses.
We write new songs
wait for spring

plan concerts in McCarren Park
        where our neighborhoods
        Williamsburg and Greenpoint
        meet on common ground.

I can show up
play my part
try to be
    a better friend
        to Pie far away
        to my new friends here
    a better grandson
        to Babcia
        by walking with her to Mass
        now that Mom and Dad don't go
        and learning her language
        so she won't be so lonely.

Pie sent me a postcard.
No note
just his address
in Puerto Rico
in a placed called Yauco.
It had a picture
of palm trees
and he drew other stuff
on top of it.
Layers
like melody
rhythm
and harmony.

It made me think
    of the trees that grow here
    a book I read
    and a song
    I started to write.

Replanted in Brooklyn's
        hard
        cold
        ground
my feet grow roots
arms, hands, and fingers
become branches and leaves
and my music
the wind
that rustles
through them
the notes **bold**
        even if
                my own voice
                is quiet
                and shy.

I tape Pie's postcard
to the wall
in the corner of Babcia's living room
that is mine.

Underneath on the bookshelf
A Tree Grows in Brooklyn
next to *The Chocolate War*
and my folded SOLIDARNOŚĆ banner

because Brooklyn *is*
the place where
I belong
and I don't disturb the universe
                        alone.

AUTHORS' NOTES AND ACKNOWLEDGMENTS

ZETTA ELLIOTT

My half of *Moonwalking* was written from the perspective of a cultural outsider. I was born in Canada in 1972; I visited family in Brooklyn when I was six or seven years old, but I grew up in suburban Toronto and attended majority-white schools. I am a mixed-race woman of African descent, but I am not Puerto Rican or Congolese. In most ways, my childhood differs from Pie's but there are some parallels. I was raised by a struggling single mother, and I spent many years both missing and resenting my Caribbean father. When he invited me to join him in Brooklyn after I graduated from college, I became an immigrant and made the United States my home. I pestered my father for information and finally went to Nevis on my own to discover what I could about our Caribbean roots. There are secrets in my family history that I am still working to uncover.

I knew that Jean-Michel Basquiat's Puerto Rican mother lived with mental illness, and I decided to make that same circumstance central to Pie's life. My paternal grandmother was institutionalized as a young woman, and both my maternal grandparents battled depression; I have a cousin who was recently diagnosed with schizophrenia, and I have lived with depression and anxiety since I was a teen. It was still challenging for me to imagine what it would be like for a thirteen-year-old Afro-Latinx boy to witness his beloved mother's psychological deterioration in the 1980s. Mental illness is too often treated as a shameful secret in families and communities of color; as we've witnessed with the COVID pandemic, lack of information paired with limited access to medical care can lead to tragedy. It was important to me that Pie had other people in his life who could help him find a way forward. The book ends with Pie reversing his mother's migration; as the Akan principle of sankofa reminds us, sometimes the only way to get ahead is to go back for the valuable things we've left behind.

When Lyn and I first decided to collaborate, this book had a slightly different narrative. Lyn finished her poems long before I finished mine, and she graciously adjusted her storyline when I decided to go in a different direction. After everything that happened in 2020, I couldn't write a conventional tale of interracial friendship. Happy endings are comforting, but I wanted my poems to provoke rather than placate. Grace Kendall patiently helped us weave our poems together and I'm thankful that my agent, Johanna Castillo, placed this project with such a gifted editor.

The pandemic altered my travel plans so most of my research was conducted at home online. Diego Echeverria's 1984 documentary *Los Sures*, available through Kanopy, was an invaluable resource for me. I took liberties with the dates of some historical events; our novel takes place in 1982 but I reference Michael Jackson's 1983 performance on Motown's televised twenty-fifth anniversary special. Michael Stewart was killed by police in 1983 but Basquiat didn't paint the works referenced by Pierre until a year later (I had the opportunity to view those paintings at the Guggenheim's "Basquiat's Defacement: The Untold Story" exhibit in September 2019). In the fall of 1982, Basquiat had a solo show on the Lower East Side but I chose to locate it in a SoHo gallery instead.

I am grateful for the support provided by my friends. Marilisa Jiménez García, Raquel M. Ortiz, Virginia Sanchez-Korrol, and Andrés Marquez shared their expertise with me, though I take responsibility for any errors in the representation of this Puerto Rican community. Ira Dworkin's book *Congo Love Song: African American Culture and the Crisis of the Colonial State* also helped me better appreciate the affinity between Blacks in the United States and the Democratic Republic of Congo.

Due to travel restrictions, it's been over a year since I've gone back to Brooklyn. The borough has changed dramatically since 1982, and I'm sure the pandemic has disrupted life in every neighborhood. Yet I also have no doubt that when I finally do return, I'll find the same glorious mix of resilient people and dynamic cultures that made me choose Brooklyn as my home decades ago. My time there made me the writer I am today, and though I wrote most of these poems in Evanston, Illinois, I hope my love for Brooklyn shines through.

LYN MILLER-LACHMANN

ON REAGAN AND UNIONS, PATCO AND SOLIDARITY

JJ is obsessed with the contradiction between Reagan's destruction of his father's union and his support for Solidarity, the union movement in Poland, where his father was born. This obsession with justice and fairness also guides JJ as he navigates a friendship with Pie despite his parents' opposition.

Ronald Reagan was a popular movie and television actor from the 1940s to the early 1960s. He first entered politics as the head of the Screen Actors Guild. His name recognition and larger-than-life personality led to his election as governor of California in 1966. By then, he had gone from a liberal Democrat, supporter of Franklin Delano Roosevelt's New Deal in the 1930s, to a conservative Republican who opposed government spending.

Reagan also became an opponent of the civil rights struggles of the 1960s and 1970s. He kicked off his 1980 campaign in Philadelphia, Mississippi, where white supremacists had murdered three civil rights activists sixteen years earlier. There, Reagan pledged to reduce the power of the federal government in favor of "states' rights," in this case a code word for pre–Civil Rights era segregation and discrimination.

Although the Republican Party had long been identified as the party of business owners rather than workers, many white workers, including union members like JJ's father, voted for Reagan in 1980. Some trusted him because he once led a union. Others wanted to roll back the gains of the Civil Rights Movement, women's liberation, and gay rights.

Reagan defeated incumbent Democratic Party president Jimmy Carter and third-party candidate John Anderson to take office in January 1981. Six months later, in August, he faced a strike by PATCO, the Professional Air Traffic Controllers Organization. The air traffic controllers wanted higher pay and shorter hours for their stressful job of keeping airplanes from colliding with one another with catastrophic results. But though the head of PATCO and much of its membership voted for Reagan, he fired the strikers, blacklisted them from further federal employment, denied them unemployment benefits, and decertified the union.

The destruction of PATCO marked the beginning of the end for unions in the United States. As workers lost the right to bargain as a group and go on strike if their demands weren't met, their wages and working conditions declined. Reagan's tax policies, lowering taxes for the wealthy and raising them for low-and middle-income people, further increased inequality.

While Reagan's policies weakened unions and workers' rights at home, he used the power of the US government to battle Communism abroad. Communism promised a society in which workers were equal and they determined their own conditions in the workplace. In reality, Communist leaders consolidated all power and property to the hands of the government. In Poland, as well as in the Soviet Union and other countries of Eastern Europe, independent unions were illegal.

In August 1980, one year before the failed PATCO strike, a strike in the Lenin Shipyard in Gdańsk, Poland, led to a national shutdown of all industries—in other words, a general strike. By the end of the month, the Communist government gave in and allowed Solidarność (Solidarity), the country's first independent union, to organize. Lech Wałęsa, a shipyard electrician who had been fired for his previous political activity, became the public face of Solidarity. But his and the other activists' victory would be short-lived. In December 1981, the Polish government backed by Soviet troops declared martial law, banned Solidarity, and imprisoned Wałęsa and many other organizers.

While PATCO never returned, Solidarity continued as a semi-underground movement supported by the Catholic Church and a growing number of Polish people. In 1989, the Communist government, facing continued strikes and economic difficulties, allowed free local elections for the first time. The following year the Communist regime fell, and Wałęsa became the first democratically elected president of modern Poland.

ON AUTISM

JJ is not diagnosed as autistic, as the criteria in the early 1980s was far more restrictive than it is today. Most diagnoses went to children who were nonverbal, and many of them lived in institutions.

In the 1980s, the diagnosis of pervasive developmental disorder, or PDD–NOS (pervasive developmental disorder–not otherwise specified) emerged to characterize children like JJ—verbal but struggling with auditory processing, spatial and motor skills, and social communication. In 1995, the diagnosis of Asperger's syndrome (AS) joined PDD–NOS and was generally used to describe highly verbal children who scored in the above average to advanced range on intelligence tests. In 2013, both PDD–NOS and AS were reclassified under the umbrella of the autism spectrum.

SOURCES

Ackerman, Peter, and Jack DuVall. *A Force More Powerful: A Century of Nonviolent Conflict*. New York: St. Martin's, 2000.

McCartin, Joseph A. *Collision Course: Ronald Reagan, the Air Traffic Controllers, and the Strike That Changed America*. New York: Oxford University Press, 2013.

Pardlo, Gregory. *Air Traffic: A Memoir of Ambition and Manhood in America*. New York: Knopf, 2018.

Tyrnauer, Matt. *The Reagans*. Four-part documentary series. Showtime, 2020.

Silberman, Steve. *NeuroTribes: The Legacy of Autism and the Future of Neurodiversity*. New York: Avery, 2015.

ACKNOWLEDGMENTS

I am honored that Zetta approached me to work on a verse novel with her. In the midst of a deadly pandemic, the novel allowed me to revisit my past and the music that was so much a part of my world then. I thank my husband, Richard, and my children, Derrick and Madeleine, for sharing their music with me.

Grace Kendall welcomed me to FSG and devoted time and care to this project. She is brilliant, and she made our work shine. I thank my agents, Jacqui Lipton and Vicki Selvaggio, who worked with Johanna Castillo to find the right home for our story. My VCFA classmate Lori Steel helped me refine my poems through multiple drafts. Krystyna Poray Goddu shared her knowledge of Polish culture and language and the experiences of post–World War II immigrants. All errors are my own. Finally, I'd like to thank David Cooper, Liz Dresner, Elizabeth Lee, Allyson Floridia, Starr Baer, and John Nora for turning a complex manuscript into a beautiful book that explores the power of art and how, through art, we can find our way home.